Angels on Holiday

by Jane Sorenson

illustrated by Kathleen L. Smith

 STANDARD PUBLISHING

Cincinnati, Ohio   24-03962

All Scripture quotations are from the *Holy Bible: New International Version,* © 1973, 1984 by the International Bible Society. Used by permission of Zondervan Bible Publishers and the International Bible Society.

LIBRARY OF CONGRESS
Library of Congress Cataloging-in-Publication Data

Sorenson, Jane.
 Angels on holiday/by Jane Sorenson; illustrated by Kathleen L. Smith.
  p. cm.–(Katie Hooper books)
 Summary: The weeks leading up to Christmas are filled with bustling holiday activities for Katie and her family, who plan to spend the special day with friends who are without family of their own.
 ISBN 0-87403-562-7
 [1. Christmas–Fiction. 2. Family life–Fiction. 3. Friendship–Fiction. 4. Christian life–Fiction.] I. Smith, Kathleen L., 1950- ill. II. Title. III. Series: Sorenson, Jane. Katie Hooper book.
PZ7.S7214Am 1989   89-4520
[Fic]–dc19   CIP
                                                                      AC

To Deln Dreffin

with love and thanks to God
for our long and special friendship

Sara Tackles Boredom

"I hate winter," said Sara Wilcox.

I set down my cup of hot chocolate on the table. "You do?"

Once my friend knew she had my attention, she really got dramatic. Tossing her red hair and rolling her eyes toward heaven, she told me, "I think I've *always* hated winter!"

"No offense," I said, "but maybe it's because you always lived in Omaha."

She sipped her chocolate. "I never thought of that. Katie, you could be right."

I grinned. "Colorado winters are different."

"Are you sure?"

"Of course," I said. "I've lived here all my life, and I've never hated winter."

She grinned too. "You never hate anything, Katie Hooper! I'll bet somebody like you could even enjoy winters in Omaha!"

"I wouldn't know," I said.

"It's true. You're never bored."

"Are you bored? Is that your problem?" I asked.

She rolled her eyes and looked up again. "It isn't me. It's life. Life is so boring!"

"Oh, get off it!" I told her.

"That's easy for you to say! I mean even after we solved the mystery of this old house, there's always something going on here."

"Such as?"

She looked around. "Such as having Silent Sam put in this new woodburning stove. I love looking in that little window at the fire! If I had a room like this, I'd never be bored."

"I think you would," I said.

"Well, maybe. But believe me, nothing ever happens at home when you're an only child! At least you have a baby sister! I can't get over how that kid changes from week to week!"

"Well, that is pretty amazing," I admitted. "Did I tell you Amy rolls over all the time now? We have to be careful she doesn't flip right off the table when we change her!"

Sara nodded. "Maybe it's just that your family's special. Your mom is always thinking something up! Has she mentioned when we can start making our quilts?"

I shook my head. My mother offered to help us make quilts. But that was weeks ago! "Mom's been acting mysterious lately," I said. "But I'm sure she'll get to the quilts eventually. Sometimes she bites off more than she can chew."

"It's OK," Sara said. "I'm an expert at handling disappointment. What's happening with your father? Has he painted anymore mountains lately?"

"He hasn't had time," I told her. "Dad's doing sketches to illustrate a children's book."

"And let's not forget Jason!" Sara grinned. "You're a lucky duck, Katie Hooper! Your brother's having a romance right before your very eyes!"

"It's not a romance," I said. "Allie Meredith and Jason are just friends. They both just happen to be interested in the environment."

Sara laughed out loud. "Get real! I've watched too much TV to fall for that! When they first meet, characters always pretend to like the same thing. Then suddenly they forget all about the environment. And it turns out they were *destined* for each other all along!"

"Were you surprised when you saw her? Allie, I mean?"

"At first I was," Sara admitted. "Frankly, I

7

thought the plot called for a blond! But I'll have to admit that she looked very pretty at the church dinner."

"That's the only time I ever saw Allie—at the church dinner," I said.

"Really?" Sara acted surprised.

"Really. Mostly they just talk on the phone."

"That's not the way it works on television," Sara said.

"I wouldn't know. And neither would Jason, since we've never had a TV."

Sara giggled. "Do you think I should tell your brother how a romance is supposed to work?"

"Maybe real life's different," I said.

Sara looked thoughtful. "I wonder how we could find out. I'd certainly like to know! Do you think we could spy on them?"

"While they talked on the phone?" I giggled.

"No! I mean if you find out Allie's coming over or something, you could let me know. And we could hide behind chairs and watch them."

"I'll think about it." But it seemed like a dumb way to keep from being bored.

Sara finished her hot chocolate. "What's happening in your room at school?"

"You mean the test in language arts?"

"Grow up!" Sara said. "I'm talking gossip! What's the latest on Kimberly Harris?"

"Nothing new," I said. After a rocky begin-

8

ning, the tall new girl in my room was blending right in. "Her mother still picks her up after school every day."

"So I've noticed." Sara sighed. "Actually, I'm afraid I've come to the wrong place. Right now, Katie, you seem as bored as I am!"

"I am not bored!" I said. "Bored is having nothing to look forward to! And I'm looking forward to plenty of things!"

"Such as?"

"Such as getting skis!" I was amazed that Sara could forget so fast. "My Friday night babysitting money is really piling up!"

"How much do you have?"

I told her.

"Not bad! I wonder if you'll ever catch up to me!"

"If it stops snowing, you'll be out of luck!" I have to be careful. I don't want Sara to know that I envy her. With her snow blower, she can do a job in no time flat! And she charges more than Jason to do a driveway!

"I guess I'm too impatient," Sara sighed. "I need something to happen right now!"

"We have a vacation coming up next week! What are your plans for Thanksgiving?"

"I don't have any," she said. "Maybe that's why I'm bored."

"None?"

"None! Zero! Zilch!" She looked toward the fire. "My mother's still the newest waitress at the restaurant. I'm not even sure if she gets Thursday off!"

"Oh, my," I said. Mom and I spend days getting ready for our big turkey dinner. I forced a smile. "Well, Sara, there's always Christmas!"

"Big deal!"

I just looked at her. At first, I couldn't say a word.

"Ho, ho, ho!" said Sara. She wasn't even smiling. "I'll admit, Christmas used to be fun when I was little. But ever since Billy Krupnick told me the truth about Santa Claus, it's been downhill all the way."

"You don't make gifts for people?" I asked.

"Are you kidding! I buy Mom a bottle of perfume. Now that my grandmother's gone, that's it." She sighed. "And, of course, Mom buys something for me. She always asks what I want, so it isn't exactly a huge surprise."

"No Christmas music?"

"Rudolph's a real bore!" she said.

"How about the carols?" I asked. "Like 'Silent Night' and 'Joy to the World'?"

"We couldn't sing that stuff at my school in Omaha." Then Sara brightened up. "But I've heard 'White Christmas' pretty often. They always include it in the television specials."

"Don't you cut down a Christmas tree?"

"Cut it down?" Sara was puzzled. "We *bring* it down—from the attic. Actually, last year we didn't even bother."

"Oh, my," I said again. I knew better than to ask about Christmas cookies. "But how about all the special things at church?" I asked. "In Omaha didn't you have candlelighting, and a choir program, and a pageant?"

Sara shook her head. "Give me a break! Until I started going with you, I never saw the inside of a church! What's a pageant?"

"It's a play about when Jesus was born," I explained. "They pick kids from the Sunday school to act out the parts. Last year, in my old church, I got to be Mary." I said it proudly. Sara didn't have to know that I was practically the only girl in the entire Sunday school.

"Who's Mary?"

"She's the mother of Jesus," I said. "It's actually the main part."

"You mean you were the star?"

"Not exactly."

"But you had the most important part?" Sara asked slowly.

"That's what I just told you."

"Then that's the part I'll audition for," Sara announced. All of a sudden, her eyes sparkled. "When are the tryouts?"

11

Lots of Invitations

Later, I had a chance to talk to Mom while I scraped vegetables for our beef stew. "If Mrs. Wilcox has to work, then Sara will be all alone for Thanksgiving. I feel so sorry for her!"

"Oh, my!" Mom said. "Why don't you invite them to have dinner with us? Then if Karen has to work, Sara can come here anyway."

I smiled. Somehow I just knew that's what Mom would say.

While the stew was simmering for dinner, I had time to call Sara. Her mom said they would be happy to accept our invitation, and Sara seemed pretty excited, too.

At supper, I reported the news to the whole family. "Guess what? Sara and her mother are coming here for Thanksgiving dinner!"

"Good," Dad said. "The more the merrier! Say, that reminds me of Mayblossom McDuff. I know she's trying to be self-sufficient. But I hate to think of her spending Thanksgiving alone up there in the cabin!"

"You're right!" Mom agreed. "Besides, it would be so much fun to have her!"

I grinned. "All right!" Mayblossom McDuff is the author who bought our cabin. Since then, she's turned into my special friend.

Jason smiled too. "I'm glad M. has decided to come to our church."

"I've been wanting to bring her home afterwards. But it never works out, because Sunday is our Family Day," I said. "Can I be the one who invites her?"

"Be my guest!" Dad laughed.

"Hey, that gives me an idea," my brother said. "There's someone I'd like to invite, too."

"Don't tell me Allie's all alone!" Dad teased.

Jason smiled. "Who said anything about Allie? I was thinking of Sam Johnson."

"Silent Sam?" I said. "Doesn't he have any family?"

"Not anymore," Mom said. "I heard that his wife died several years ago."

"Maybe that's why he's so quiet," I said. "Maybe he's just sad."

"Or maybe he never did talk much," Jason said. "Not everybody blabs all the time like you do, Katie."

I just ignored him.

"Jason, I think inviting Sam is a wonderful idea," Mom said. "You can call him after supper."

"It looks like we'll have a big family this year," Dad said, smiling. "I'll have to try to find the extra leaves for the table."

"And we'll have to get a bigger turkey," Mom said.

"Just be sure there's plenty for leftovers!" Dad told her. Actually, he says that every year.

"Don't worry!" Mom smiled. "Having leftovers is the best part of eating turkey at home!" And that's what she says every year!

The first time I dialed her number, M. wasn't at home. I let the phone ring eleven times.

My brother had better luck with Sam Johnson. "He's coming!" Jason said. "He sounds happy!"

"What did he say?" Mom asked.

"I bet I know," I laughed. "He probably said, 'Hmmmmmmmm'!"

Jason laughed too. "You called it, Katie! But then he thanked me and said he'd be honored to come."

"Poor Silent Sam," I said. "Maybe we can be his family."

14

"He sure helped us out!" Dad said. "This stove is going to save us a lot of money!"

"And besides," Mom said, "the first floor of this old house is finally warm!"

I tried M.'s number once more before I went up to do my homework. This time she answered.

"This is M. McDuff," said a peppy, cheerful voice.

"And this is K. Hooper!" I said. I smiled as I heard her peel of laughter.

"Katie! What a wonderful surprise! How are you?"

Just hearing her speak my name made me feel happy right down to my toes. "I'm fine," I said. "How are you?"

"Couldn't be better!" she said. "I looked for you Sunday, but I didn't see you with your family. I hope you weren't sick."

"I've been working in the nursery," I told her. "Mrs. Stone was late picking up David."

"What can I do for you?" she asked.

"My family wants you to come here for Thanksgiving dinner. Do you think you can?"

"How wonderful!" M. said. "Actually, I was just starting to feel sad that I'm so far from my friends in the East! I'd love to come!"

"Good!" I said. "This will give you a chance to meet my friend Sara. She's coming. And maybe her mother, if she doesn't have to work. She's a waitress. And Silent Sam's coming. He's the one who put in our woodburning stove. See, Mom was on Dad's case because it was practically freezing in here." I took a deep breath.

"Whoa, Katie!" M. laughed. "Let me have a turn! I want to invite you for that overnight we talked about. Can you come up to the cabin Saturday and spend the night? I can bring you back down the next morning for Sunday school."

A huge smile spread over my face. "What time? I'll ask Mom."

It was all arranged. Dad would drive me up in Purple Jeep. If the weather was good, he'd go on up to Flat Rock to paint.

"You know what?" I asked Mayblossom.

"No, what?"

"I think this just turned into the best day of my life!"

M. laughed. "I'm glad! I love you! See you Saturday!"

"I love you, too!" Still grinning from ear to ear, I hung up the telephone. I hesitated just a second and then dialed Sara's number.

"Hello," said Sara.

"It's me, Katie Hooper," I said. "Guess what? Thanksgiving is really going to be special! You're going to get to meet Mayblossom McDuff. And Silent Sam!"

"I already met Silent Sam," she said. "Don't

you remember? The day your father dropped the couch on his foot! He told me I reminded him of a famous actress."

"Oh, sure," I remembered. "What was her name?"

"Phyllis Diller," Sara said. "But you're right about Mayblossom McDuff. I haven't met her. Naturally, I've heard you talk about her. Who could forget a name like that!"

"You'll like her!" I said.

"I hope so," said Sara.

"There's something else, Sara. Mom says you can help us fix the dinner. On the day before, we make pies and cranberry sauce. And Thursday morning we stuff the bird!"

"Wow!" said Sara. "Now that is something!"

"Have you ever stuffed a turkey?"

"Are you kidding!" she said. "I've never even seen a whole turkey. Except in pictures."

"I can't believe it!"

"Katie, you know what? I just realized something. I don't hate winter anymore!"

I smiled. "I think you just needed something to look forward to," I told her. "Sara, I'm glad you're coming over."

"It sounds like a real family gathering." Sara paused. "To be honest, all my life I've dreamed about spending a holiday at a real family gathering."

Suddenly, Jason was standing next to me and pointing to the telephone.

"I have to go now," I said. "See you at the bus stop!"

"Katie, I thought you were going to talk all night!" Jason said.

"I hardly ever talk on the phone," I reminded him. "I suppose you just want to call Allie."

"So what if I do?"

"I'll bet you wish your friend could come here for Thanksgiving!" I teased.

"Frankly, it never even occurred to me," my brother replied. "I want to tell her I found an article in the paper about water pollution."

A Babysitting Challenge

My Friday night babysitting at Stones' has turned into a regular routine. Now, Mrs. Stone doesn't even ask me if I'm available. She just tells me what time Mr. Stone is coming to pick me up.

And once I get to their house, that's pretty routine also. David, the baby, usually has been fed and put in his crib. And Doris, who's three, meets me at the door begging me either to read her a book or play *Chutes and Ladders*.

But this week was different.

"Right on time, I see," Mr. Stone said. He's the only person who ever uses our front door.

I smiled as I snapped my down vest. "I'm bringing a new game for Doris."

"I don't know," said her father, once he started the car. "Doris has been giving us a hard time this week."

"What's wrong?"

"Her jealousy of the baby seems to be getting worse," he said. "I'm afraid she's spent most of the week being punished in her room."

When Doris didn't come to the door, I figured that's probably where she was. In her room, I mean. And I was right.

"Well, hi, David!" I said.

The baby, who's exactly Amy's age, was lying in the playpen in the center of the living room. He looked up at us and smiled a toothless grin.

"He's so cute!" I said. "And I've noticed at church that nothing seems to bother him."

Mr. Stone shook his head. "Very different from Doris. She was never easygoing like this—even when she was a baby!"

"Mom says every child is different," I said. I couldn't think of anything else.

Mrs. Stone came out of her bedroom wearing a red dress. She was trying to stick an earring into her right ear, but she couldn't find the little hole. She smiled. "Hi, Katie!"

"Hi, Mrs. Stone."

Walking to the top of the stairs, she called down to Doris, "OK, Doris! Katie's here. You can come out of your room now!"

We could barely hear the child's reply. "I'm not coming!"

Mrs. Stone shook her head. "Katie, I'm sorry to leave you with Doris acting like this. But I'm sure you'll cope. If not, the phone number where you can reach us is in the kitchen."

"I'll be fine," I said bravely. "Sometimes kids are better once their mothers leave."

After I heard the car pull away, I sat on the floor and played with the baby. "Hi, David! Give me a big smile!"

He acted like he knew what I was saying. Waving the rattle I put in his hand, he grinned from ear to ear.

After a few minutes, I decided to pick David up so I could start getting him ready for bed. As I lifted him, he pushed his little feet against the padded playpen. I was impressed! My sister still hasn't figured out what her legs are for!

I heard Doris's door open, but I pretended I didn't notice. Soon she stood right next to me.

"David's a wienie," Doris said.

"What's that?"

She didn't smile. "I think it's like a nerd. I heard it on television."

"Babies aren't nerds," I said.

"Katie, I never said he was a nerd," she told me. "I said he's a wienie."

Oh, well. The grinning baby couldn't care less.

Why should I? "Want to help me put your brother in bed?"

"No," she said. "But I'll watch you do it." I changed the baby's diaper, slipped him into his sleeping bag, and laid him in his crib.

"It's OK to close his door," Doris told me. "It gets hot in our house. Did you know our stove is called 'super hot'?"

I shook my head. "Is that because your parents just put wood in it?"

"No," Doris said. "My *parents* didn't put wood in it. My father did. My mother doesn't understand about wood stoves."

She didn't see me grin. We walked out and sat down in the living room.

"I'm glad when he goes to bed," Doris said. "The wienie, I mean."

"Did you know I have a baby sister the same age as David?" I asked.

"Is she a wienie?"

"No, she isn't," I said. "When Amy first came home from the hospital, she slept most of the time. But now she's awake more. Is that what's happening with your brother?"

Doris nodded. "I wish we could send him back!" she said. "He's a big disappointment!"

I didn't let myself smile. "Doris, I brought you a game. If you get all ready for bed first, I'll show you how to play it."

Doris smiled for the first time. "I'm good at games. I bet I'll win!"

"You might!" I told her. "You really are very good at games, Doris. But don't forget, tonight you can't cheat!"

"How come?"

I had to think fast. "It's not fair. It's a bad habit. If you cheat, other people won't like you."

"Who cares!" she said.

I shrugged my shoulders. "I guess we aren't going to be playing the game anyway. I don't see you getting ready for bed."

She scurried off down the stairs. "You'll see, Katie Hooper!" she yelled over her shoulder. "You'll be surprised!"

The Stones live in a bi-level house. Upstairs is the living-dining room, kitchen, the parents' bedroom, and David's nursery.

Once I think the baby's asleep, I usually go downstairs. That's where the woodburning stove is, in the family room. At the other end of the lower level is Doris's bedroom.

Now, as I followed her downstairs, I could see what Doris meant about the temperature. This house is much warmer than ours. I suppose it's because Home Sweet Home is such a barn of a place. Why, we've got closets bigger than these bedrooms!

In record time and smiling from ear to ear,

Doris soon joined me in the family room.

I pretended to be astonished. "Why, Doris," I said, "you just broke the world's record!" She loved it!

But then, just as we got the game all set up, David began to cry.

"Ignore him!" Doris pleaded. "It's my turn! Katie, it's my turn now!"

"I can't," I tried to explain. "David's just a little baby. Something could be wrong."

"I hate the little wienie!" she yelled. She raced to her room and slammed the door.

I ran upstairs and opened David's door. Immediately I saw what had happened. The baby had wiggled himself into a corner of the crib, and his head was wedged next to the bumper pad.

"Hey, you little gymnast!" I laughed as I pulled him back into the center of the crib. "Don't you know you're too little to be doing tricks like this!"

While an old tear rolled down his cheek, David looked up at me and grinned.

I found Doris lying on her bed sobbing. "I hate him! It isn't fair! The stupid little wienie! I'd like to send him back to wherever he came from!"

"David's OK now, Doris," I said.

Finally, she stopped crying. She looked up at me. "Katie, can I go home with you?"

I shook my head. "Your parents would miss you. They'd feel awful!"

"I'll be so good," she pleaded. "I promise."

"Your mother wants me to come here to your house every Friday night," I said. "That's even better."

She seemed confused. "Well, maybe."

Once we got to it, the game was a big success. Well, actually, Doris did cheat a couple of times. But what's the difference? She'll learn!

"Katie, will you listen to my prayer?" Doris asked. It was the first time she'd asked. To be honest, I felt honored! I sat on the edge of her bed and closed my eyes.

"Dear Lord, thank You that Katie's my baby-sitter," she said. "And thanks for letting me win the game." She paused, and for a second I thought she was finished. Then she continued. "Lord, I have a special prayer. Please take my brother back! In case You forgot, his name is David Anthony Stone. But please don't tell my parents who gave You the idea! Amen."

When I opened my eyes, Doris was staring at me. "You won't tell, will you?"

I shook my head. "You'll change your mind," I told her. "Doris, you won't always feel this way!"

"Wanta bet?"

"No." I smiled. Suddenly, I decided to give her a hug. "Doris, I'm glad you're my friend."

"Really?" she said.

"Really!"

Doris smiled and wriggled down under the covers. She didn't even ask for another drink of water.

"Goodnight, Doris," I said softly. I turned out the light. As I left the room, her words came out of the darkness. "Katie, I love you!"

Well, naturally, I felt even better than terrific! I wished I could tell somebody, but Sara wouldn't understand. Smiling to myself, I took out my book and sat down in the family room to read.

After a couple of chapters, I started getting sleepy. I shook my head, walked around a little, and finally went upstairs.

And at exactly ten o'clock I went into the kitchen and took a Pepsi from the refrigerator. But don't worry! Mrs. Stone said I could!

My Very First Overnight

I woke up Saturday morning so exhausted I couldn't even move. But then I discovered that January was sleeping on top of my feet.

"Hey, Lazybones, I have to get up," I told him. "I can smell breakfast!"

I grinned as my dog opened one eye, thumped his tail twice, and rolled over. "Actually, you're better than an extra blanket!" I told him. To be honest, although my room now looks nicer, it still gets pretty cold up here.

January jumped off the bed and headed for the stairs. He's so stupid, he probably thought I said I was ready to take him out!

"Later!" I told him, but he just stood there. "You'll just have to wait until I get dressed."

When I got down to the kitchen, my father was eating the first pancakes all by himself. Jason, who's supposed to be helping him cook, was talking on the phone.

Dad, wearing his special apron, sat alone at the table. "Couldn't let them get cold! Where is everybody this morning?"

Jason hung up the phone. "Katie, your dog needs to go out."

"I can see him," I said.

"Hey, guys, I thought our pancake breakfast was supposed to be a family tradition," Dad grumbled. "Where's your mother?"

"She's upstairs nursing the baby," I said. I slipped on my vest. "I'll be back in a minute."

"This is ridiculous!" Dad said. "Some togetherness! What happened to the good old days?"

"Oh, Dad!" Jason said. "Not that again!"

When we finally assembled at breakfast, Dad announced that he and I would be leaving right after lunch for our trip to Divide.

I spent the entire morning doing my chores and getting ready to go. Actually, I changed my clothes three times—from jeans to skirt, and back to jeans again. Also, I packed and unpacked my suitcase three times.

"You look fine," Mom told me. "Don't forget. You'll need clothes for church tomorrow."

"I know," I said. "Mom, I'm not a baby!"

"Did you put in clean underwear?"

To be honest, I hadn't! When she wasn't looking, I did.

During the drive to the cabin, I was so excited I hardly said a word.

"Sometimes I can't believe we really live in Woodland Park now," Dad said. "I feel as if it's a dream, and when I wake up I'll be back inside the cabin."

I hardly heard him. "Right, Dad," I said.

Later, when Purple Jeep turned into the lane, I watched a thin curl of smoke coming out of the chimney. It was the sign of home I'd watched for all my life. "I can't believe we don't live here anymore," I said.

I looked over at Dad. He just nodded.

As I climbed down from the car, something seemed wrong. I tried to figure it out. Everything was so quiet.

"Want me to come in with you?" Dad asked.

I shook my head. "I'm OK. I'll see you in the morning!" Bravely I picked up my suitcase and began to walk. There was no sound except my feet crunching. When I reached the door, I turned and waved. I could see Dad waiting and smiling.

I reached up and tapped the doorknocker. Nothing happened. I banged it harder the second time.

Suddenly, the blue door opened and I nearly tumbled inside.

"Katie!" Mayblossom said. "I can't believe it! I didn't hear you at all! I was just coming out to check the mail."

Once I saw M., I felt lots better. I turned and waved to Dad. We watched him wave back before he turned Purple Jeep around and headed off.

"It's so quiet," I said. "Is something different?"

"I don't think so," she said. But then she began to laugh with her tinkling giggle. "I'll bet I know what it is! Everytime we've seen each other before, January has howled."

"That's it!" I laughed. "It's been almost a kind of signal."

"I guess I didn't tell you to bring January, did I?" she asked.

I shook my head. "Was he invited?"

"No matter," M. said. "But it would have been fun! Please come inside. Here, let me help you with that suitcase."

I hung my jacket on my old peg next to the door. But now, instead of being next to Jason's vest, it was hanging beside M.'s navy sweater.

"You keep the cabin so neat," I said. "It was lots messier when we lived here."

"Living alone has its advantages," Mayblossom said. "Oh, I have water boiling. Katie, be-

31

fore we do anything else, let's have a cup of tea!"

I didn't tell her that I never drink tea.

She smiled. "Would you like sugar?"

I didn't know what to say. "Do you put sugar in yours?"

"No, I don't," she said.

"Then I won't either."

It tasted awful. I tried hard not to make a face like I do when I take medicine. "This is delicious," I told her.

"You're faking it, aren't you, Katie?"

I grinned. "How did you know?"

"Here, I'll get you some juice!"

The hardest part of unpacking was getting my suitcase up the ladder to the loft. Laughing hysterically, we both finally made it into what is now M.'s guest room. When my family lived here, it used to be Jason's room. Now it contains twin beds with matching blue comforters.

"Which bed is mine? Does it matter?"

"Not at all." Mayblossom smiled. "While you hang up your clothes, I'm going in to turn off my computer."

Frankly, I had only one thing to hang up, so it wasn't a big deal. Afterwards, I joined M. in what used to be my room. Now it's where M. McDuff writes her books.

"How's your book coming?" I asked.

"Fine," she said. "I usually don't do any writing on Saturdays, but I got an idea after lunch. I guess I can't hear the door when the computer's running."

"January would bark," I said. "Maybe you need a dog."

"It's funny you should say that, Katie," M. said. "The thought has crossed my mind. I'll admit that I do feel alone up here. I've never really lived in the country before."

"It's too bad my dog doesn't have a brother!"

"Right," Mayblossom said. "I could call him February!"

"You know what?" I said. "I just realized that I don't miss this room so much anymore! My room at Home Sweet Home got painted white. And Mom even stenciled hearts around the top. That's my symbol, you know."

"Can I see your room when I come for Thanksgiving?"

"Sure," I said. "I'll even pick it up!"

M. laughed. "I'd hate to have you do anything so drastic!"

I laughed too. "It's OK. Mom says we have to straighten up the whole house. Well, not the *whole* house. But any place where Mrs. Wilcox and Silent Sam and you might look!"

"You're talking about Sara's mother?"

"That's right," I explained. "It turns out that she doesn't have to work at the restaurant after all. But Mrs. Wilcox is an immaculate house-keeper. And Mom's really nervous!"

"And who is Silent Sam?"

"He's the guy who installed our woodburning stove. Maybe you've seen him at church. He has curly white hair, and he takes huge steps. His name is really Sam Johnson. He doesn't talk much, so I call him Silent Sam."

M. laughed. "I don't think I've noticed anyone with that description!"

"We think his wife died," I added. "He's actually very nice."

But I don't think M. heard me. She looked like she was thinking about something else.

We Hike
in God's Country

With both of us laughing like little kids, May-blossom and I climbed back down the ladder.

"Katie, is there something you'd especially like to do?" she asked.

"To be honest, it's fun just being here!"

M. smiled. "It's fun for me, too! But isn't there anything you miss? Something you did here that you can't do in town?"

"We could take a walk!" I said. "January and I used to hike all over the place!"

"Excellent!" M. said. "As a matter of fact, I try to walk every afternoon myself. Let's go now! It gets dark so early these days."

For her age, Mayblossom is in pretty good shape. I thought maybe I'd have to take it real slow, but she surprised me. We headed off past the shed and the row of pine trees.

"Have you discovered the cave?" I asked.

"No! Is it near here?"

"I thought that's where you were heading."

She shook her head. "I've walked this way before, but I've never seen a cave! It sounds like an adventure!"

"Follow me," I told her.

As we reached the trees, the ground was patchy with occasional leftover snow. After a few minutes, I led the way down an almost-hidden path. "It's right down here!"

But when I reached my destination, I stopped and just stood there looking. "I can't believe it! It got smaller!"

Mayblossom's tinkling laugh made me smile. "How long since you've been here, Katie?"

I tried to remember. "Not that long! Well, I guess it's been almost a year! It doesn't even look like a cave, does it?"

"It looks kind of like a cave!"

I giggled. "Be honest, M.! It really looks more like a shelf!" We climbed underneath. "Sometimes I used to eat my lunch down here."

M. grinned. "Surprise!" She pulled out two apples. But to be honest, picnics are more fun when it's warmer.

"Would you mind if we headed over to those

rocks?" M. asked. "I was up there the other day. When you stand between those two big ones, there's a spectacular view of the mountains!"

I smiled. "I know." I felt glad that she had discovered it for herself. I can still remember the first time I climbed up there with January!

When we reached the rock formation, I scrambled up. Mayblossom, wearing her pink jogging shoes, was right behind me.

At first neither of us said a word. We just stood together and looked. "This truly is God's country!" I said, finally.

M. agreed. "If God really has a country, it must be like Colorado!"

We walked more slowly on the way back. I thought about all the times I had been out here all by myself. Well, I couldn't actually go alone until I got my dog. "Sometimes when we took walks, January used to run ahead and try to flush out birds," I remembered.

"It's really too bad you didn't bring him," M. said. "He would have enjoyed this too!"

"Would you really want a dog like January?"

"Sure. Dainty little dogs really aren't my type," she said. "I think I prefer big ones—like collies or German shepherds. But I've never really had room for a big one."

I nodded. "Big dogs need to run. Do you get lonely taking walks all by yourself?"

She shook her head. "I never think about it. I'm always busy looking at things. And I do have to watch so I don't get lost!"

"Do you take walks when it snows?"

"I have cross-country skis," M. told me. "Don't you?"

I shook my head. "We used to have some old beat-up ones when I was little. But once we got Purple Jeep, nobody in our family used them anymore. I don't know what happened to them."

She was surprised. "I thought everybody in Colorado skied."

"Not everyone," I said. "Dad's always discouraged us. He says skiing is a rich person's sport." I looked over at M. and decided to share my dream. "You know what? Sara and I are saving up for downhill skis!"

She smiled. "How close are you?"

"I really don't know," I said. "How much do they cost?"

"Beats me! But I think we could find out!"

When we got back to the cabin, I helped M. make a fire in the big stone fireplace.

"It was nice of your father to leave all that firewood," she said.

"Thanks. Well, to be honest, at first he didn't have any way to bring it with us!"

M. laughed real hard. "Now that you have your wood stove, you probably could use it."

"No," I said. "Dad says you need it worse!"

Our supper was actually more like a party! Mayblossom set up a small table right near the fireplace. We had blue placemats and big blue candles stuck into shiny silver holders. And we even used real cloth napkins!

At first, when I spread my napkin on my lap, I wasn't feeling very sure of myself. "I'm nervous! What if I spill something on it?"

Mayblossom just laughed. "Then I'll just throw it in the washer!" Then she got serious. "Katie, let's pray!" I bowed my head.

"Lord," she prayed, "thank You for giving Katie and me the blessing of friendship! Please bless this food and our time together. Amen."

I opened my eyes and watched Mayblossom pick up her fork. I copied her and took my first bite. "Wow!" I said. "What's this?"

She smiled. "I'm glad you like it! It's called Chicken a la King."

"I think I just tasted something that wasn't chicken," I told her.

She smiled. "I'll bet it was a mushroom."

"I never ate a mushroom before."

"That's one of the fun things about eating out," she told me. "Trying new things, I mean."

"Can you give me the recipe?"

"You're a cook?" She seemed pleased when I nodded.

We even had dessert. It was dark chocolate in a little kind of cup. It has two names. The one that made me laugh was "Mousse." If God eats dessert, this is probably His favorite!

I was surprised to discover that the kitchen now contains a dishwasher! "May I push the button? I've never tried a dishwasher before."

"Of course," M. said. "I had someone from the Springs put this in. Once you get used to one, it's hard to do dishes by hand."

"There's one more thing, M. I notice you have a television."

"Is there a favorite program you'd like to watch, Katie?"

"I don't know. We've never had a TV."

"Really!" She showed me how to change the stations. Eventually, we decided to watch a game show. She was pretty good at it. But I don't think they even knew we were playing.

Later, at bedtime, I felt kind of shy. I was glad I had packed a robe. Finally, I came down to use the bathroom.

"Goodnight, Dear!" Mayblossom gave me a hug. "Katie, thanks for coming!"

I hugged her back. "It's been the best day of my life!"

I climbed the ladder, turned, and waved down to her from the loft. Then, leaving the guest room door open a crack, I curled up in the bed next to the wall. But I couldn't sleep.

Finally, I got up and stood at the window. There wasn't a sound. The moon was so bright, I could see everything for miles around. Actually, the view was the same one I had looked at all my life. But now something is different. I don't live here anymore.

"Sometimes growing up is hard," I told the Lord.

I Feel Real Cool

"Katie!" The voice was gentle. When I opened my eyes, Mayblossom was standing next to my bed. She had a big smile on her face.

"What do you know! I'm still here!" I said. "What time is it?"

"Time for breakfast! I have a nice little fire going. Let's eat breakfast in our robes!"

I grinned and bounced out of bed. At my house, we never eat in our robes!

"Would you like to pray this morning?"

"Sure!" I bowed my head. "Lord, thank You for this time here with M.! Please bless the food. And don't forget, Lord! You'll have to help all the Sunday-school teachers today! In Jesus' name. Amen."

Mayblossom went into the kitchen and returned with our plates. "I hope you like eggs Benedict!"

"Eggs who?"

M. laughed. And in the next few minutes, I discovered another new treat. "You're sure a good cook!" I told her.

"I'll have to admit that I don't usually fuss this much just for myself," M. told me. "Cooking is lots more fun when I have guests!"

"Am I really your first guest?"

"The first who stayed overnight! And that's special!" She smiled at me.

Although I wished our breakfast together could go on forever, the time came when we had to get dressed. "Why don't you use the bathroom first," she suggested.

"Sure," I said. "Compared to sharing a bathroom at my house, this should be a cinch!"

At last we were ready for church. First, M. told me how nice I looked, and then I told her how nice she looked. She really did!

As we left through the front door, I took one last look around the cabin. For some reason, this morning I didn't feel particularly sad.

Together we walked down to the shed.

"Wow! I like your car!" I told her. "I'm surprised. I thought you'd have something more . . ." I couldn't finish my sentence.

M. grinned. "Something more dignified?"

"I guess so. Boy, wait until Jason sees this!"

Mayblossom McDuff's car is low, shiny, and bright red! I sat in the front seat. Since there isn't a back seat, it was my only choice! When M. turned the key to start the motor, an antenna shot up. Suddenly, we were surrounded with the sound of violins!

"Wow! This is really something!" I said.

"It is fun, isn't it?" She smiled.

"What's the car's name?"

"It's 'Wimsey,'" she told me. "That's the name of a character in one of my favorite books."

M. turned and we zoomed onto the highway. "You know what?" she said. "I bought Wimsey as a present to myself on my fiftieth birthday."

"You bought yourself a present?"

She laughed. "Why not? I didn't think anyone else would buy it for me!"

I laughed too. "You're probably right!"

She seemed to be enjoying the ride as much as I was. "Since I moved out here, I've been thinking maybe I should get myself a four-wheel drive or a pickup truck!"

I couldn't believe it. "But what would happen to Wimsey?"

"Don't worry," she assured me. "I'll never get rid of Wimsey! He's a member of my family!"

"That's a relief!" I actually felt glad!

44

Mayblossom glanced at me and grinned.

Frankly, I've never given any car a second thought. But now I realized something! This is a far cry from riding around in a purple jeep! Suddenly, I started to feel cool. In fact, real cool! For the first time in my life, I—Katie Hooper—actually felt cool! I found myself wishing Sara could see me! I grinned. Maybe I'd even get myself some sunglasses!

Since on Sunday morning there's practically no traffic, we made excellent time. In fact, that was the problem! We were nearly the first ones in the church parking lot. Not even one kid saw me arrive in that cool red car!

"I've never come in time for Sunday school," M. told me.

"Want to visit my class?"

She smiled. "I guess that's a possibility. Do you know if there's a class for adults?"

"Yes, there is," I told her. "It's a big class! That's where Mom and Dad go every week."

To be honest, I just wanted to hang around out there next to Wimsey! But in my heart I knew it was too cold. M. and I went inside and stood near the table where Mr. Upjohn greets everybody.

In a few minutes, Harry Upjohn showed up. "Well, good morning, Mayblossom!" He smiled and shook her hand. He didn't seem to notice that I was there. "It looks like you're here in time for Sunday school!"

M. smiled back. "I brought Katie Hooper down. She spent the night with me at the cabin."

"Well, good!" he said. He glanced at me and smiled. But then he turned back to M. "I think I just have time to take you down to our classroom. Come with me and I'll introduce you to our teacher!"

M. looked very happy. "See you later, Katie," she said.

I just stood there and watched the two of them head down the hall.

In the next five minutes, the building got so crowded that Mr. Upjohn could hardly make his way back to his table.

Although I kept watching for my family and Sara, I didn't really expect to see them. In spite of Jason's efforts to get us here on time, we usually straggle in during opening exercises. And Sara, of course, rides with us.

As the crowd thinned and people headed off to their classrooms, I followed along. When I slipped into my row of chairs, the other kids looked surprised. My teacher nearly fainted.

"Katie, you're on time!" Jennifer said.

I grinned.

During the second verse of "Stand Up, Stand Up for Jesus," Sara arrived. With her red hair

46

sticking up in every direction, she stood there rolling her eyes. As she made her way to Mrs. Pearson's class, everybody laughed. Everybody, that is, except Mrs. Pearson!

Sara and I are in different Sunday-school classes. Although I got credit for bringing her the first week, after that someone decided she'd be better off in the other class. The problem is that Sara asks too many questions! Personally, I don't think my teacher had a clue about how to handle her!

This morning, just before we were dismissed to go into our classes, Mrs. Smedley walked to the front. "Next Saturday morning, we'll be starting practice for the Christmas pageant!"

Well, I'd like to tell you that everybody cheered, but that isn't true. To be honest, some kids actually groaned! I couldn't believe it!

"Now, now," said Mrs. Smedley. "Let's not be so immature!"

Sara's hand shot up.

"Yes?" said Mrs. Smedley. Since she doesn't actually teach in our department, I don't think she even knew who Sara Wilcox was. At least, she didn't know then!

"Do I understand that you're announcing the tryouts?" Sara said. Somebody giggled.

"As usual, all of you will have parts in the pageant," Mrs. Smedley told us.

"I'll be Baby Jesus!" said a large boy whose name I don't know. More giggles.

Well, you could just tell that Mrs. Smedley wasn't born yesterday. "That will do!" she said. Her voice was quiet and firm. Suddenly, the room was silent. "I'll expect to see you in the gymnasium Saturday at ten o'clock!"

"I'll be here!" Sara told her. Nobody else said a word.

We Stuff the Bird

"Mrs. Hooper, nobody believes I can cook Thanksgiving dinner!" Sara said. "Especially my mother!"

"You'll see," Mom told her. "It really isn't that hard!"

"Are you positive?" Sara asked. "I don't think my mother knows that!"

"Maybe *her* mother didn't know it either!" Mom said. "But you and Katie can pass along the good news to *your* children!"

By the time Sara got to our house Wednesday afternoon, Mom had cleared the usual clutter from the kitchen. She was ready for action!

"Will I need an apron?" Sara asked. Until recently, she didn't even know what an apron was!

"You girls can start with the cranberry sauce," Mom said. "While you're doing that, I'll roll out the pie crusts."

"I always thought cranberries came in cans!" Sara laughed.

"Not at our house!" I told her.

Sara and I worked together at the sink, picking out the bad berries and tossing the good ones into the colander to be washed. She was slow at it. "Isn't it hard for you to decide which ones are OK?" she asked.

"Nope!" I said. "It's not that big a deal!"

Next, we took a large pot and measured in four cups of sugar and four cups of water. We heated this until it boiled. Then we dumped in the washed berries.

"See how easy it is!" I said.

"Well, it's easy all right," Sara said, as she watched the berries floating around. "But I have to be honest! This sure doesn't *look* much like cranberry sauce!"

"Of course not!" I said. "Now we just have to cook it until the cranberries pop open!"

Soon we were spooning hot cranberry sauce into two big bowls. "It gets even thicker when it cools off," I told her.

Mom was just finishing the third and fourth pie crusts. "The trick is to handle it *lightly*," she explained. "Pie crust won't be flaky if you treat

the dough like a lump of modeling clay!"

We watched Mom shake some flour onto the table and her rolling pin. Gently, she rolled a ball of dough into a large circle. When she lifted it onto a pie pan, it hung over the edges.

"Easy does it!" Mom said. "Now, we're home free!" Well, we really weren't. But it didn't take her long to shape the dough into a little rim around the edge of the pie plate.

"Can we bake the scraps of dough?" I asked.

"Sure," Mom said.

I took all the extra pieces and put them on a small cookie sheet. "Here, Sara," I said. "Just sprinkle some sugar and cinnamon on top!"

"How much?"

"There's no recipe!" I told her. "Here, watch me!"

"So what kind of pies are we making?" Sara asked. "Cherry?"

"Cherry!" I said. "For Thanksgiving?"

"Well, pardon me!"

"Oh, my," Mom laughed. "I guess we do get used to our own family traditions. On Thanksgiving, we always have pumpkin, because that's what *my* mother fixed! But this year, with so many guests, we're adding a couple of pecan pies."

Sara smiled. "Where's your jack-o'-lantern?"

I just looked at her. "Jack-o'-lantern?"

"You know. The pumpkin for the pies!"

"We use canned pumpkin," Mom said.

"Canned?" she laughed. "You actually use canned! I can't believe it!"

"Making pie fillings is lots easier than doing the crust!" I told Sara. All we had to do was follow the recipes and measure carefully.

While Mom watched, Sara and I mixed together in a bowl the canned pumpkin, milk, eggs, sugar, and spices. Next, for the pecan pies, we needed eggs, sugar, corn syrup, and melted butter. And, of course, pecans!

"We don't even have to bake the crusts first," Mom said. "We're going to put the filling right in the raw crusts!"

"How come?" I asked.

"For certain pies, the crust and fillings bake together at the same time," Mom explained. "You should always check your recipe."

Although the pies smelled delicious, naturally we couldn't taste them. Sara and I did enjoy eating our sugared scraps of pie crust. Baked a few minutes, they tasted almost like cookies.

"Want to see the bird?" I asked Sara.

"What bird?"

"The bird! You know—the turkey!"

"No, girls! Not until tomorrow!" Mom said. "Sara, can you be here by eight o'clock? It's a big turkey, and it will have to bake a long time!"

"I'll be here!" Sara said.

And she was! On Thanksgiving morning, Sara arrived while I was still eating breakfast. She smiled. "I can't wait to see that big bird!"

Silently, we watched as Mom unwrapped the huge turkey and placed it in a pan on the kitchen table.

"How come it's so white?" Sara asked.

"That's the way turkeys always look before they're put in the oven," I explained.

"He looks kind of naked, doesn't he?"

Mom laughed. "You're right Sara. He does! He's also kind of empty. Let's get started on that stuffing!" She brought over a huge bowl full of bread cubes.

"This is bread? How did you get it shaped into those little squares?" Sara wondered.

"It comes like this," Mom told her. "See, the directions are right on the package. I just add some extra celery and onion."

Mom gave Sara and me each a knife and a cutting board. "You can cut up several stalks of celery. I'll do the onions myself. I don't want you girls crying!"

"Why would we cry?" Sara asked.

"You've never cut up an onion, have you?" I said. "Mom, let her see for herself!"

But Sara had to take our word for it! She isn't exactly handy with a paring knife! I mean, she even had trouble cutting up the celery!

"Sara, for your first time, you did great!" I told her. Mom grinned and winked at me.

We watched as Mom gradually poured the hot liquid over the bread mixture and kind of stirred the bread around.

"Yuck! What did you say this is going to be?" Sara asked.

"Dressing!" I told her. "You know, the stuff that's inside the bird!"

Her eyes got big. "That's where dressing comes from? Inside the bird?"

"Of course," I said. "Well, first we have to put it inside."

Sara shuddered. "I had no idea," she said. "This actually turns into dressing?"

"It does," Mom assured her. "The juice from the turkey flavors the bread mixture."

"I had no idea!" she said again.

"Trust us!" Mom laughed. "Here, want to help stuff it in?"

"Sure!" Sara picked up a big spoon.

"Pack it in loosely," Mom told us. "Dressing expands as it bakes."

"Look how cute he sits there!" Sara giggled. Mom held the bird up in a kind of sitting position, and we spooned dressing into the neck cavity.

But as I pinned the flap of skin against the

turkey's back, Sara winced. "I can't believe it," Sara said. "Do you have to do that?"

"Of course," I said. "Otherwise the dressing would fall right out!"

Mom laid the bird down again and held his legs apart so we could put dressing into the lower cavity. Sara's eyes got big. "This is embarrassing!" she said. "Mrs. Hooper, are you sure it's OK for me to watch this?"

I giggled. All my life I've just taken this whole process for granted!

Sara and I spooned in dressing until no more would fit. Then Mom laced the hole shut and tied the bird's legs together.

"Hold him up, Katie, while I bend back the wings!" Mom said. She has this way of tucking the wing tips in back of his neck.

"Well, at last the bird looks comfortable!" Sara laughed.

"That's all there is to it, Sara," Mom said. She loaded the roasting pan into the oven.

"There's still the basting," I remembered.

"Don't let the word fake you out, Sara!" Mom said. "That just means squirting the bird with juice so he doesn't dry out."

"Can I baste him?" she asked.

"Sure," Mom said. "Come back over in about an hour!"

"He'll be starting to get brown!" I told her.

"And the smell! Well, you'll see!"

Sara put on her jacket. "You know, you're right, Mrs. Hooper! Fixing Thanksgiving dinner isn't really such a big deal!"

"You and Katie were lots of help!" Mom said.

Sara grinned. "Someday, when I get my own family, I'm even going to teach all the neighbor kids how to do it!" She paused. "You know. Just in case their mothers can't!"

Our Family Gets Bigger

Although the delicious smell of turkey was the same, it seemed strange to be celebrating Thanksgiving in a different house! This is our first real holiday in Home Sweet Home. And many of our old ways of doing things had to change.

Dad and Jason had just finished putting all the leaves in the dining room table. But now it took up the entire room.

"No problem!" Dad told Mom. "When we finish eating, we can just go into the keeping room."

"I guess we'll have to," Mom said. "I just hope it won't be too cold in there." Even I could tell that her usual enthusiasm was missing.

"I want you to be happy, Elizabeth!" he said.

"Can't we have a real fire in the other fireplace—just this once?" I asked. "It won't seem like Thanksgiving if we don't have a real fire!"

"And let all that heat go up the chimney?" Dad said.

"That's why Sam Johnson put in this woodburning stove!" Jason said.

But Mom began to smile. "Katie's right, Steve! That's the solution, all right! If we can have a nice fire in the keeping room fireplace, this arrangement will be perfect!"

Dad started laughing. "Somehow, I don't think Sam will approve!"

"Leave that to me! I'll handle Sam!" Mom said. And nobody doubted that she would!

Now, with our guests due any minute, the house was all straightened up. To be honest, it looked neater than it had since we moved in. Whatever couldn't be put away had been hidden! We were ready for inspection!

The first person to arrive was Mayblossom McDuff. "What a beautiful family!" She smiled at us. "And what a charming old house!"

I hugged her. "Want to see my room?"

"Of course, Katie! In a minute."

"Let her get her breath!" Dad said.

M. squealed. "Guess what! January didn't even howl!"

Everybody looked at the dog. January just

stood there looking at M. As a matter of fact, he looked exactly like he was smiling!

"Amazing," Dad said. "I never thought I'd live to see the day!"

"Me either!" I laughed.

After we hung up M.'s coat, she followed me upstairs to my room. "How lovely, Katie!"

I smiled proudly. "The stenciled hearts look nice, don't they!"

She winked. "And everything's so neat, too!"

I giggled. "Didn't you say you wanted to meet my dolls? Actually, now that I have Sara, I hardly ever talk to them anymore!"

Well, I was just introducing M. to Audrey when we heard the noise. *AaaaaOoooooooooo!* It was January's howl! He sounds like he's singing the "Star Spangled Banner"!

"Oh, dear," Mayblossom said. "It must have taken him a few minutes to realize I'm here!"

As we headed for the stairs, I heard Sara's voice. "Either he stops that, or I'm going home!" *AaaaaaaaOooooooooo!*

"Katie, come down here!" Dad yelled.

"Don't talk like that, Sara," Mrs. Wilcox was saying. "It isn't polite!"

I'm not sure what happened next. I think it was Silent Sam knocking at the back door. But the oven timer also went off and the baby started crying! You get the picture!

"Oh, my!" Mom laughed. "Happy Thanksgiving, everybody!"

With a start like that, how could the day help being fun! By the time we finally got the dog quiet, we were one big, very happy family!

Mom, a huge smile on her face, took charge. "Steve, before you carve the turkey, could you please carry it around so everyone can see it!"

"Wait until you get a load of this, Mom!" Sara said. "I did the basting all by myself!"

"I hope she wasn't a nuisance, coming back over here so often!" Mrs. Wilcox said.

"Don't be silly! We couldn't have fixed the dinner without her!" Mom told Sara's mother. "Karen, could you help with the ice cubes?"

"Of course!" Mrs. Wilcox seemed pleased to have something to do.

"And Mayblossom, I need some extra hands to make the gravy!" Mom said.

"I'd be honored!" M. told her.

"Now, Sam!" Mom gave him her biggest smile. "By chance, have you had experience mashing potatoes?"

"Hmmmmmmm," he said, as his face turned red. "How did you know?"

"It was just a lucky guess!" Mom laughed. "But we could sure use a strong arm!"

"And Katie and Sara, would you girls mind dressing Amy? She can wear that little pink outfit I laid out on the dresser!"

"And Jason, I need you to be in charge of putting the chairs around the table!"

There was a buzz of excitement as everyone headed off to fulfill their assignments.

Upstairs, I showed Sara how to put on Amy's dress. Getting it over her head isn't the easiest! But when we finished, the baby looked darling!

"Amy looks almost like *your* sister, Sara!" I said. "Your pink jogging shoes match!

Are these the ones Mom and I gave her?"

"It's the first time she's worn them!"

"You little doll!" Sara told her. Amy smiled and blew a little bubble!

"Come on," I said. "Let's go downstairs!"

Naturally, everybody rushed over to greet Amy! And, when they had time, they took turns holding her and making her laugh. Amy loved it!

Before dinner, everybody stood around the table and held hands in a big family circle. Dad led the singing: "Praise God, from whom all blessings flow!"

Thanksgiving dinner was fabulous! I don't think anybody enjoyed the meal more than Sara! Her eyes got big as she tasted each item — cranberries, turkey, dressing, and both kinds of pie. Although she didn't say a word, she beamed with pride as everyone said it was the best turkey dinner they had ever eaten!

"I'm too full to move! I'll never eat again!" Dad announced.

"He always says that!" I giggled. "But later we always find him picking at the bird!"

"I could use a walk!" Mayblossom said, when we finished in the kitchen. "Katie, would you and Sara like to show me the neighborhood?"

"Sure!" I said. The three of us giggled our way down toward Sara's house.

"I was walking right about here when I saw the ghost!" Sara explained.

"No!" Mayblossom said. "Tell me about it!"

Well, by the time we got back, my two best friends knew each other.

Later, everybody made their way into the keeping room and cozied in by the fire. On Thanksgiving, Dad always makes us go around the circle and tell why we're thankful. Last year, he got real upset because Jason groaned!

But all that was forgotten now. "I have an idea," Dad said. "Let's go around the room and tell why we're thankful!"

"How nice!" M. said. "May I begin? I'm thankful that the Lord brought me safely to Colorado. And I'm especially thankful that I can celebrate Thanksgiving with all of you!"

Actually, each person said pretty much the same thing! Silent Sam was last. "Hmmmmm," he said, smiling. "Today is so special! I haven't felt this much love in several years! I'm thankful to spend Thanksgiving as part of a real family!"

Suddenly, I realized that Silent Sam was talking! Maybe he realized it himself, because then he leaned back in his chair, smiled, and said, "Hmmmmmmm"!

"It's strange," Mom said, "but today reminds me of the wonderful family gatherings we had in Illinois, when I was growing up! You know, we Hoopers need some aunts and uncles and cousins!"

"You've certainly made us feel a part of your family!" Mayblossom said.

"I have an idea!" Mom said. "Why don't you all come back here for Christmas dinner!"

"What a wonderful invitation!" M. said. "Maybe we could draw names so we'd each get a Christmas gift!"

"Now she's my kind of woman!" Dad laughed. He loves presents! "It will be a secret! We won't tell anybody whose name we get!"

"Hmmmmmm!" Silent Sam said. Everybody laughed.

In no time flat, Dad had written all our names on pieces of paper and mixed them up in his green golf hat. "It was your idea. You go first, Mayblossom!" he said.

"Oh, this is so exciting!" she squealed. We watched her squint at the name and then put the paper in her purse.

Dad continued passing the hat around the room. "Keep it a secret!" Sara reminded us.

When my turn came, I reached in. I peeked at the name on my paper. Then I looked up and grinned. But, naturally, I didn't tell!

Before everyone left, we stood together by the fireplace and huddled together in a gigantic family hug! And then it was time for our guests to go home. Thanksgiving was over!

But ten minutes later, I found Dad in the kitchen picking over the turkey bones. I guess Mom's right. Some things never change!

Pageant Practice

When I got to my babysitting job Friday night, I discovered that Doris had had another bad week. As long as her brother was up, she wouldn't come out of her room!

"I've tried everything!" Mrs. Stone said. "But Doris refuses to be in the same room with him! I don't understand it! David is so lovable!" The baby grinned his toothless little smile.

"Maybe I'll have better luck," I told her. Frankly, I was confident that once her parents left, Doris would come out. I was wrong.

"Why would you want to stay in here all by yourself?" I asked her later, after I had tucked David in for the night.

"I don't like him!" she said.

"Why not?"

"I don't know. I just don't!"

We played our old stand-by, *Chutes and Ladders*. Surprisingly, Doris never cheated once! "Doris, you're getting to be such a good sport!" I smiled at her.

"I want you to like me, Katie!"

"I do like you! Do you want me to listen to your prayers again?"

She shook her head. "Katie, it's no use praying! As you can see, the kid's still here!"

"I think Jesus wants you to start loving David," I told her. "Have you thought of that?"

"Yes, I have," she said.

"Well?"

Her face was serious. "Once he's gone, I'll probably like him fine!"

I figured it was useless to argue with her. And in the end she did let me hear her prayers. This time, she recited the standard list, asking God to bless everyone—except her baby brother!

On the way home, Mr. Stone asked, "How was Doris?"

"She was OK," I said. "I'm sure she really does love David. She just doesn't know it yet!"

Before I went to bed, I tucked some more baby-sitting money into the box on my desk.

* * * * * * * *

On Saturday morning, my father dropped Sara and me off at the church on his way into town to run some errands. We were the first kids there.

"Do you think I have a chance to be Mary?" Sara asked.

"I don't know," I said. "This is much bigger than my last church. There are lots of girls, and only one Mary."

"I've always wanted to be a star!"

"Have you ever been in a play?" I asked.

"Well, not really."

I grinned. "Sara, if we were both angels, I bet we'd have lots of fun!"

"I doubt it!" Sara said. "I mean, angels sound pretty boring to me!"

"Well, that was just an example!" I told her. "Maybe we could both be shepherds."

"What do they do?"

"They watch sheep. At least, that's what they do until the angels come. Then they go to see the new baby in Bethlehem." I looked up. "Here comes Mrs. Smedley!"

Quite a few other kids, mostly girls, had joined us in the gymnasium. But I could tell that not everybody was here. Not by a long shot!

If Mrs. Smedley was disappointed in the turnout, she didn't let on. "Good morning, boys and girls!"

"Good morning, Mrs. Smedley," said a blond girl I don't know.

Sara whispered to me, "It figures! I bet that girl just wants to be Mary too!" Now Sara turned to the front and said, "Wow, Mrs. Smedley! You're some knockout in that dress!"

Mrs. Smedley looked confused. And all the kids looked at Sara. Sara just stood there and smiled.

"Well, now," Mrs. Smedley said, "as you probably know, you young people in this department are the backbone of our Christmas production!"

I wondered what she was talkng about.

"Let's start with the angels," Mrs. Smedley said. I glanced at Sara. She was rolling her eyes.

"Now, I know most Christmas pageants feature preschoolers in angel costumes." Mrs. Smedley smiled like she knew a secret. "But I realized years ago that little angels might be cute, but they usually can't carry a tune! That's where you boys and girls come in! And, of course, there is one speaking part!"

When she heard the words "speaking part," Sara perked up.

"So, we'll need a number of Senior Angels with nice singing voices. And we'll also need a Chief Angel to announce the good news!"

Mark Morrison tossed a paper airplane, which landed at Mrs. Smedley's feet. She ignored it.

Mrs. Smedley looked down at her paper. "I also have speaking parts for a Chief Shepherd and an Innkeeper." She looked up again and smiled. "And I've always been able to count on your department to give me a nice group of shepherds."

"That's it?" Sara asked.

Mrs. Smedley hesitated. "Well, naturally, the entire department will also sing a carol and recite a Scripture passage."

"I'm going home," Sara whispered.

"You can't," I whispered back. "Dad won't be back to get us for over an hour!"

Sara sighed.

"Those who want to try out for the speaking parts can give me your names after we practice our song."

Sara raised her hand. "Somebody told me that the starring role in this production is a character named Mary!"

"I suppose you could say that." Mrs. Smedley smiled. "But, of course, Mary doesn't really *say* anything."

"She doesn't?" Sara asked. She looked at me.

"I never told you Mary *said* anything!" I whispered.

"Then how can Mary be the star?" Sara asked.

"You don't know the story?" Mrs. Smedley asked.

"Are you kidding!" Sara bluffed. "Why, everybody knows the story! Just tell me who gets to be Mary."

Mrs. Smedley smiled again. "Actually, the role of Mary hasn't been assigned yet. But we usually choose an older girl. Someone from junior high or high school."

"Oh!" Sara said. She turned to me. "So, how come?"

"I have no idea!" I whispered. "Maybe it's because Mary's going to have a baby!"

Sara's eyes got big. And she forgot to whisper. "No kidding! Is that what this is all about—having a baby?"

Everybody laughed.

Immediately, Mrs. Smedley took control. "It isn't funny!" she said. "All of you, just think about this for a minute! Here was Mary, about to have her first baby. Does somebody give her a baby shower? No! Suddenly, just before the baby's due, she's ordered to travel to Bethlehem on a donkey! Just because somebody wants to count all the Jews in the country!"

The kids had simmered down.

"And when Mary and Joseph finally arrive in Bethlehem, nobody will even give them a hotel room!"

Now Sara was listening carefully.

"They have no choice. They end up out in a

barn with the animals!" Mrs. Smedley said. "And that's where the baby Jesus is born!"

"So, where were these angels? Just hanging out in the barn?" Sara asked.

"Probably some were," Mrs. Smedley laughed. "But, in our pageant, the angels go out to tell the shepherds that a Savior has been born! Afterwards, the shepherds decide to see for themselves. And, of course, they find the baby Jesus!"

Nobody said a word. Not even Sara.

Mrs. Smedley looked at her watch. "In the time we have left, I want to hear you sing the angels' song. Those who aren't chosen as Senior Angels will automatically become our shepherds. And, don't forget! If you're interested in a speaking part, see me before you go home."

During the singing, I thought Sara was acting like she couldn't wait to get out of there. When Mrs. Smedley pulled me over to stand with the best singers, she hardly seemed to notice.

But once we were dismissed, Sara was the first one to stand in front of Mrs. Smedley.

"I want to try out for Chief Angel!" Sara told her.

"And what's your name?"

"Sara Wilcox." She was very serious. "To be honest, Mrs. Smedley, I really wanted to be a star. But I've decided I'm willing to do almost anything to get my career rolling."

Mrs. Smedley laughed. "I'll see what I can do, Sara." She turned to me.

"I'm Katie Hooper. I'm one of the Senior Angels," I reminded her. "But if you need one, I can recommend a real cute baby!"

"Thank you for the suggestion, Katie," she said. "But in our church we've always just used a doll."

The Name I Picked

Once Thanksgiving's over, there's no stopping Christmas from coming! It's like a big snowball that just rolls down the hill faster and faster!

Frankly, I don't know about everybody else, but Hoopers don't just go out and buy Christmas presents. We make them. It's a family tradition. Don't worry! I started on mine weeks ago! Last year I let it go to the end, and I learned my lesson the hard way!

But this afternoon, as I sat in my room knitting on my father's scarf, I thought about my problem. Oh, not with the scarf! It involves the name I picked from Dad's hat on Thanksgiving. I got Mayblossom McDuff! Since it's a secret, please don't tell!

It isn't that I can't think of an idea. As a matter of fact, I've known from the beginning exactly what I want to give M.! But her Christmas present isn't something I can make. You see, I'm getting her a dog!

As I thought about it, I realized this was a perfect thing to pray about! I put my knitting down on my lap and closed my eyes. "Lord, I can just picture M. taking a walk with her new dog! You probably can too! Can You see what he looks like? I think he's big! Am I right?"

I sat there waiting. "Now, please don't take this the wrong way, Lord! I honestly don't mind that January's stupid! He gives our family lots of laughs! But, since Mayblossom's up there in the cabin all alone, I really think she needs a dog that's smarter! Do You agree?"

I opened my eyes, then closed them again. "Sorry about that, Lord! I almost forgot the most important part! Just exactly where am I going to find this dog? Please help me!"

I opened my eyes and purled two stitches. And suddenly I realized I don't have much time. For finding the dog, I mean.

Downstairs in the kitchen, Mom was spooning applesauce into Amy's open mouth. My sister looked just like a bird! "Have you looked out the window, Katie?" Mom asked. "The snow is really coming down!"

76

"Sara must be happy!" I said. "She's been praying for deep snow! I hope she has plenty of gas for her snow blower!"

"Personally, I hope it stops by tomorrow," Mom said. "For Family Day we're going up to Cochrans' to cut our Christmas tree!"

"Good!" I said. "Hey, aren't Family Day plans supposed to be a secret?"

Mom winked. "So don't tell," she laughed.

"Mom, I've been trying to figure something out. Do you know where I could get a dog?"

Mom laughed. "Don't tell me you've decided to trade January in on a new model?"

I shook my head. "It's not for me. It's for Mayblossom. I already had the idea. And then I picked her name for our Christmas party!"

"Hey, aren't the names supposed to be a secret?"

I copied her wink. "So don't tell!" I laughed.

"A dog's a pretty expensive gift!" Mom said. "I thought you were saving for skis!"

"Actually, I wasn't planning to spend much," I admitted. "Are dogs ever free?"

"Sometimes," Mom teased. "Take January, for instance!"

I giggled. "How about smart dogs?"

"It depends. Sometimes pedigreed dogs can cost hundreds of dollars!"

"Wow! It's a good thing I prayed!" I said. "I just

77

know there has to be a cheap dog for Mayblossom somewhere! Mom, where can I look?"

"You might try the classified ads," she said. "Last night's newspaper is in that pile over there. Unless I wrapped the garbage in it."

The classified section was right on top. I carried it up to my room and spread it out on my bed. Once I found the things for sale, I was fascinated! I mean, there was an electric train with a village mounted on a big board! And three tickets to a rock concert in Denver on January 6. And a whole wardrobe of ladies' dresses, size 8.

Finally, I found a listing called "Pets and Livestock." I passed up the AKC whippets ("exotic toy greyhounds"), the ginger-colored cat ("lovable, long-haired"), and the Maltese puppies ("tiny balls of white fluff").

But I put checks in front of some others:

GERMAN SHEPHERD PUPS (male) AKC excellent quality, good temperament.

GOLDEN RETRIEVER AKC males and females. Champs. Eyes clear.

BEAUTIFUL ADULT COLLIES for adoption. Good home. Family raised.

And then I saw it!

78

FREE. Irish setter, male AKC, 7 years old, good temperament.

I rushed back down to the kitchen. "I found one!" I told Mom. "I'm going to call about it right away! Warn me if somebody comes in!"

An Irish setter would be perfect! "Please, Lord!" I prayed, as the phone rang. But I was too late! The man who answered was sorry, but "Champ" was already in his new home. And the man was tired of getting calls!

Although I felt disappointed. I still had the other numbers. One by one, I called them. The cheapest dog was over 200 dollars!

"I had no idea!" I told Mom. "Can you believe almost 500 dollars! Just for a dog!"

"Not just any dog," Mom said. "You're talking about one with papers!"

"Well, at least I have a start! I'll ask around at school. And I'll keep looking in the paper."

"I'll keep my ears open, too!" Mom promised.

"You know what?" I laughed. "January's starting to look pretty good!"

The following morning, Mrs. Smedley was back in our Sunday-school department. "I'm happy to announce the names of those with special parts in our Christmas pageant!"

She looked down at her paper. "Senior Angels—Michael Moreland, Katie Hooper . . ."

I didn't hear the other names. It was pretty dumb, but I felt a grin spreading over my face!

Next came the shepherds. Only kids who came to yesterday's practice knew that the list of shepherds included everybody else who showed up! Except, of course, for the speaking parts! Mrs. Smedley continued. "This year's speaking parts have been awarded to the following: Chief Angel—Sara Wilcox; Chief Shepherd—Angela Jones; Innkeeper—Mark Mahoney. Congratulations!" Mrs. Smedley smiled. There was weak applause. Very weak.

Mrs. Smedley looked around the room. "I know some of you must feel disappointed. But I have good news! Everyone will get to participate in a choral reading from Matthew. And you'll all be learning four stanzas of 'Joy to the World'! Let's make this the best Christmas pageant our church has ever had!"

"You sure look happy," I told Sara after Sunday school was over.

"I can't wait to get on the set!" she said. "A real actress makes the most out of every part." She grinned. "To be honest, I think I was born for character roles! After all, I've never really thought of myself as just another pretty face!"

I giggled. "You're a character, all right!"

"Come on! We'll be late!" she said. And we headed down the hall to the church nursery.

My Brother Rebels

On the way home, I told my family what had happened. "Guess what! Sara and I were both chosen as angels in the Christmas Pageant!"

"But not just ordinary angels!" Sara said. "Actually, Mr. and Mrs. Hooper, you can be very proud of your daughter! Katie's a Senior Angel!"

There was a pause. I knew Sara expected me to tell them about her part. "And Sara's the Chief Angel!" I said.

"Wow!" Dad said. "How about that!"

"Actually, it's a speaking part!" Sara said.

I kept waiting for my brother to make some smart remark. But he didn't!

"I suppose you'll have to go to practices," Mom said.

"Saturday mornings at ten," I reported.

"How about costumes?" Mom asked. "Have they said anything about costumes?"

I looked at Sara. "I don't think so. Did Mrs. Smedley mention costumes?"

She shook her head. "Do you think there's a Costume Department taking care of that?"

Mom laughed. "I've found that usually the Costume Department is staffed by *mothers!*"

"You're awfully quiet, Jason," Dad said.

"I have something to ask you," my brother said. "Do I have to spend this afternoon with the family? Allie Meredith wants me to go with her to hear a talk about acid rain."

I was so surprised I nearly fainted!

"But, Jason, you know Sundays have always been our Family Day," Mom said.

"And today is extra special," Dad told him. "I'm sure you didn't realize it, but we're all going to the farm to cut down our Christmas tree!"

"Katie can help," Jason said. "You don't need me!"

"But it won't be the same without you!" I told him. "We've always done it together every year! It's a Hooper Family Tradition!"

"Frankly, I think I'm getting too old for all this family stuff!" my brother said. "Don't forget, next year I'll be in high school!"

Sara was watching with great interest. When

we got to her house, I could tell she didn't want to get out of the car. "Let me know how this turns out!" she whispered.

After Sara left, Mom was the first to speak. "I'm really disappointed to hear you talk like that, Jason," she said. "Your father and I have always tried to put you first! A lot of parents don't do anything with their children."

My brother didn't say anything.

"Don't argue with him, Elizabeth!" Dad said. "He's coming with us, and that's final!"

Now nobody was talking! Except for Amy's gurgling, the inside of Purple Jeep was quiet.

"Allie's going to call," Jason said, as we walked into the house. "So, is the answer 'no'?"

As Dad stood there in the kitchen with his coat on, a funny look came over his face. "I just realized something," he said. "I'm sounding exactly like my own father! That's how he always talked to me."

Mom walked over to Dad. "Jason, why don't you give us a little time to think this through."

"What if Allie calls?" he asked.

"Tell her you'll call her back," Dad told him. "Elizabeth, let's go into the keeping room. Katie can take care of the baby."

Well, personally, I was pretty upset at my brother! I didn't even look at him. "Who gave you the right to ruin Christmas!"

"Don't exaggerate, Katie!" he said. "Christmas is going to happen no matter what they decide! Nothing can ruin Christmas!"

When Mom and Dad returned, they were serious but calm. We all went into the keeping room and sat near the woodburning stove.

Dad began. "Jason, we thought you and Katie might like to know how our Family Day got started."

"When we first got the idea, we did it to try to make Sundays special," Mom said.

Dad looked very serious. "My father never spent time with me. I wanted to be sure I didn't make the same mistake with my children."

"But a family tradition isn't a law," Mom said. "It can be changed! Traditions have to keep serving their original purpose. There's no point in continuing one if it's driving us apart!"

"Right," Dad said. "After all, one reason Jesus gave us Sundays was for special times of loving and happiness!"

"But I still love the family," Jason said. "I guess I'm confused."

"Well, your mother and I want to try to work something out," Dad said. "One possibility is to continue having Family Day, but let you invite your friends to join us."

"Yeah!" I yelled. "Wait until I tell Sara!"

"But if Sara's always included, then it won't be

84

our family any longer," Jason said.

Mom smiled. She didn't say anything.

"We'll just try some changes and find out what works," Dad said. "In a few weeks, we can have a meeting to see how everybody feels."

"Jason, would you like to invite Allie to come with us this afternoon?" Mom asked.

"I sure would!" Jason was smiling now. "I'll call her right away!"

It sounds silly, but we all kept talking so we wouldn't hear what Jason was saying on the phone.

"Can we bring the small hatchet?" I asked. "I'm no good at swinging that big one! And then Jason gets to do most of it!"

"Fine," Dad said. "If we can find it!"

"Just think! It's Amy's first Christmas!" Mom said.

When Jason returned, he did not look happy.

"What's wrong, Jason?" Mom asked.

"Your plan won't work!" he said. "Allie doesn't want to come with us!"

"Oh," Mom said. "Did she tell you why?"

My brother looked down. "She told me her family doesn't even celebrate Christmas!"

I was stunned. Personally, I always thought everybody was into Christmas!

"Then you'll just have to choose, Jason," Dad told him.

"I guess I did already," my brother said. "I'm coming with you guys!"

"Great!" I said.

Everybody tried to act as if nothing had happened. After lunch, Jason and I were alone in the kitchen doing the dishes. "Were you surprised about Allie?" I asked.

"Kind of," Jason said. "We've never really discussed Christianity. I realized Allie didn't go to church. But I'm proud to have her for a friend. Everybody at school likes her."

"She came to our church supper!" I remembered.

"But she wasn't really comfortable," Jason said. "She'd rather talk about the environment."

"There'll be other things to do with her. The environment's going to be here a long time!"

Jason shook his head. "I have a feeling I'm history! Allie told me if I didn't want to go with her, she'd get someone else!"

"So, big deal!" I said. "I'm sure there are lots of other girls who'd appreciate a guy with experience cutting down Christmas trees!"

"Katie, you're all right!" He smiled. "Thanks for listening!"

I nearly fainted again! But I didn't let on. I just grinned. "Hey, what are sisters for?"

Actually, it turned out to be one of the best Family Days we've ever had! The fresh snow

86

made everything look like one of Dad's mountain paintings. Amy even got to hold her first snowball!

After a very long and involved discussion, we finally chose a tall fir tree. Everyone took turns chopping. But then Mom got the idea that she also wanted to decorate another smaller tree! Dad couldn't believe it!

"I've got an idea!" Jason said. "Let's see if Katie can cut this one down all by herself with her little hatchet!"

With everybody cheering, I did it! As long as I live, I'll always remember that homely little tree! (Later it ended up in our keeping room!)

It really was a perfect day. And I, for one, was glad my brother didn't miss it! As we all sang carols on the way home, I glanced at Jason and smiled. So what if he didn't see me!

Jason Joins the Cast

When we walked into the house, the telephone was ringing. It wasn't the first time that's happened.

"How does Allie do that?" I asked.

"Beats me!" As Jason dashed to answer it, a smile spread across his face. But the ringing stopped just as he got there.

Dad stuck his head in the door. "Elizabeth, where do you want the trees? On the porch?"

"I'll help you, Dad," Jason said. "And then I'll call Allie back."

I was setting the table for supper when my brother made his call. It was a quick one. In fact, he hardly talked at all.

"What's up?" I asked.

"It wasn't Allie! She said she didn't call me!" he said.

"Oh?"

"She said she had someone there and couldn't talk to me. I could hear laughing."

"Maybe it was her family," I said. My brother didn't say anything. I noticed he had stopped smiling.

I hate to see Jason so sad. "Getting the trees sure was fun, wasn't it?" Even as I heard myself saying it, somehow it sounded dumb.

"Sure, it was!" Jason said. "But that doesn't change the fact that I've lost my only friend!"

"Maybe you'll find others if you aren't spending so much time with Allie."

"Shut up, Katie!" he said. "If I want a sermon, I'll go to church!"

I shut up. Nobody ever said being a younger sister was easy!

During supper, the telephone rang again. "Someone else can get it!" Jason said. "No way is it going to be for me!"

But he was wrong!

"Yes, this is Jason Hooper," he said. Now we all listened.

"Who did you say this was?" He looked puzzled.

"Oh, sure. Yes, Katie mentioned you!" Now *I* was puzzled!

"You're kidding!" he said. "No, I don't even know her!" Aha! I thought. Something about a girl!

"I don't know," he said. "I'll have to think about it. Can I call you back?"

When he returned to the table, I tried to read the expression on Jason's face. Actually, I couldn't. He didn't look happy, sad, or even surprised. Without a word, he came back to the table and just sat down.

There weren't many dishes. It was my turn to wash. I decided I wasn't going to ask Jason anything. For sure! If Jason didn't want to talk about it, it was all right with me!

"It was Mrs. Smedley," he said, finally.

"Mrs. Smedley!"

"Isn't she the one in charge of the Christmas pageant?"

I nodded. "Right!"

"You won't believe this!" Jason said. "She asked me to be in it. She wants me to be Joseph."

"Joseph!"

"She needs somebody tall. And somebody told her I'm the only one in our department taller than Jessica Hotchkiss."

"Who's Jessica Hotchkiss?"

"I have no idea," Jason said. "But she must be tall. She's the one they picked to be Mary."

"Is she nice?"

90

"I said I don't know her! To be honest, I don't know any of the kids."

"That's impossible, Jason!" I told him. "We've been going to this church for months!"

"I know the first names of the guys in my Sunday-school class, and that's it!" Jason said. "There's a clique, and I'm not in it!"

"What did you tell her?" I asked. "Mrs. Smedley, I mean."

"I said I'd let her know."

"Are you going to do it?"

"I might."

The next morning, I could hardly wait to tell Sara! "Guess what happened? Jason and Allie aren't an item anymore!"

"You mean she dumped him?"

"You could put it that way," I said. "But guess who's going to be Joseph in the Christmas pageant!"

"Not Jason! Wow!" Sara said. "This could be even more exciting than I thought! I can't wait to get on the set!"

"I know who's going to be Mary!"

"Who?"

"Her name's Jessica Hotchkiss."

"Maybe next year," Sara said.

"Did Mrs. Smedley give you your part to learn?"

Sara nodded. "I have it right here."

Somehow the Christmas story looked different typed on a piece of paper stuck in Sara's notebook! But as I read it, the words were familiar:

"Do not be afraid. I bring you good news of great joy that will be for all the people. Today in the town of David a Savior has been born to you; he is Christ the Lord. This will be a sign to you: You will find a baby wrapped in cloths and lying in a manger."

"That's the point where I start singing," I told Sara. "When you say 'lying in a manger.'"

"That's your cue? How do you know?" Sara asked. "Did Mrs. Smedley tell you?"

"I've heard the story before," I told her.

That night I was so busy with homework, I almost forgot to check the newspaper for dogs. Actually, it was Mom who reminded me on Tuesday night. "Speaking of dogs," she said. "You also forgot to feed January!"

I spread the newspaper out on my bed again. This time I knew exactly where to look, and I didn't get sidetracked by other ads.

The "tiny balls of white fluff" were still in there, along with the German shepherds and golden retrievers. The only new ad was for a two-year-old Newfoundland that needs lots of room and love. But the price was $250! I didn't even bother to call.

The week went fast. Before Christmas, they always do! In my spare time, I worked on Dad's scarf. I'm not really sure Dad needs a scarf, but that isn't the point. I already know he's going to love it! We Hoopers always appreciate everything we get. We know each gift has been made with lots of love!

I was rushing around Friday night when Mom showed me a new dog ad. It was a long one:

> FOR ADOPTION. Blend the eager-to-please temperament of a shepherd with the people-loving personality of a Lab and you get an extra-nice young gentleman named RALPH. Neutered, housebroken, well-trained, obedient. Gets along well with other dogs and cats, too.

The ad had been placed by something called the Animal Shelter. Since I couldn't reach the number before Mr. Stone arrived to pick me up, I took the ad with me. I read it to him on the way to his house. I wanted to ask him if I could use his phone to call.

"I think this dog sounds nice," I told him. "But whoever heard of a dog named RALPH!"

"I wonder if Ralph gets along with children?" Mr. Stone said.

I was surprised. "Are you looking for a dog?"

"Well, I wasn't," he said. "But maybe a dog

would be just the thing for Doris!"

"Now that's an idea!" I said.

"Don't mention it to her," Mr. Stone said. "I think I'll talk it over with my wife. Would you mind if I took that ad?"

Actually, what could I say?

After her parents left, Doris acted about the same as usual. I didn't make a big deal out of her staying in her room. It was her choice.

"Come on, David!" I said, as I picked up the happy baby. "It's time to get ready for bed!"

I pulled off David's wet diaper. As I turned to put it in the diaper pail, I held the baby with my left hand so he wouldn't roll off the table. Mom had taught me how to do it, and now I don't even think about it anymore.

But when I turned back, I saw that David was sending a spray straight across the room! "Oh, no!" I laughed. "Mom forgot to tell me that baby-sitting for boys is different than for girls!"

Later I gave the children a good report when their parents came home. "Doris was fine," I said. "She didn't cheat once at *Chutes and Ladders,* and she let me hear her prayers again."

Mrs. Stone smiled. "We think maybe Doris needs something to take her mind off the baby. First thing in the morning, we're going to call about Ralph! Thanks for the idea, Katie! We'll let you know what happens."

We Take It From the Top

As usual, Jason helped Dad make pancakes on Saturday morning. But not once did Dad crow about them as a Family Tradition! I've always thought being a Hooper was so special! Now, suddenly, we're on the verge of turning into just another boring family! And frankly, it's Jason's fault!

"I don't know why I ever said I'd be in the Christmas pageant," my brother announced. "I really should be working on my semester science project!"

And, believe it or not, nobody teased Jason or told him to snap out of it!

"Katie, see what you can find out about the costumes," Mom said. "If I have to do that on top of everything else, I'd at least like to know about it!"

I couldn't believe it. Mom never complained! Was my life going down the drain? It was almost a relief to head for pageant practice!

On the way to church, my brother sat in the front seat. He and Dad talked about getting wood for our new stove. Although Jason looked up and said "hi" to Sara, he continued to make his point. "I still think we should drive up to Cochrans'!"

"If we have to, we will, Jason," Dad said. "But I'd still like to find a closer place!"

I looked at Sara and smiled. "So, have you memorized your part?" I asked.

"Not exactly," she said. "It's been a very busy week."

When we got inside the church gym, nothing was happening. Mrs. Smedley wasn't even in sight. Three boys were playing tag. The rest of the kids, mostly girls, were hanging around in small bunches. Jason didn't know what to do. He didn't want to wait with Sara and me, but he didn't have a choice. "I hate this!" he said.

"Merry Christmas!" I laughed.

Suddenly, Mrs. Smedley marched in, and her smile warmed the room. "Good morning!"

"Good morning!" Sara said. It sounded like she was the only one.

"OK, let's get this show on the road!" Mrs. Smedley's voice snapped everyone to attention. "I was just talking on the phone to our narrator," she said. "Unfortunately, Mr. Stone is tied up and can't rehearse with us this morning. But we'll manage. We'll just pretend I'm Mr. Stone."

A couple of kids giggled.

"I bet I know where he is," I told Sara. "He's checking out a dog named Ralph!"

"Please give me your attention!" said Mrs. Smedley, looking right at me. "We're going to begin with the Three Kings. One of our Wisemen has to leave early because of an appointment at the orthodontist."

"Do you need Mary?" asked a tall girl, who had to be Jessica Hotchkiss. I poked Sara.

"Yes, I guess we do," Mrs. Smedley said, looking up. "And where is our Joseph?"

My brother looked as if he'd like to drop through the floor. "Right here," he gasped. Awkwardly, he made his way to the front.

Mrs. Smedley had arranged two chairs in the center of the stage. Jason followed Jessica up the stairs, and they took their seats. Mary and Joseph never once even glanced at each other!

"So that's who got the part!" Sara whispered. "No wonder! She looks like a model!"

"Well, personally, I think she looks awfully tall and thin," I said.

"Don't be stupid, Katie! That's what models are supposed to look like!" Sara told me.

"Oh!" I hate it when she puts me down. "Actually, the real Mary might not have looked like that at all! Think about it! Would the real Joseph look exactly like my own brother?"

"I suppose you're right."

We had to hand it to Mrs. Smedley. She knew exactly what she wanted! Now the only trick was to get the three Wise-men to walk slowly enough. "It isn't a race, you know! It took them *years* to get all the way to Bethlehem! You really must come in with more dignity!"

"The director's right," Sara said. "Besides, if they walked that far, they probably were pooped!"

"It's hard to get the effect when they're just dressed in jeans," I explained. "It looks lots better when they're wearing their bathrobes!"

"All right!" Mrs. Smedley said. "Let's take the Luke story from the top!"

"What's that?" I asked.

"She means from the beginning," Sara said.

"I'll need the innkeeper!" Mrs. Smedley looked at her paper. "Mark Mahoney! Where is Mark Mahoney?"

"He isn't here!" someooe yelled.

Mrs. Smedley shook her head. "All right, then. Mary and Joseph, you can take a break.

Let's have all the shepherds and angels up here on the stage!"

"That's us!" Sara said. She led the way.

There are lots of shepherds! They filled most of the stage. "Stand closer together, Shepherds!" Mrs. Smedley said. "All right, quiet now!"

Mrs. Smedley began to read:

And there were shepherds living out in the fields nearby, keeping watch over their flocks at night. An angel of the Lord appeared to them, and the glory of the Lord shone around them, and they were terrified.

The shepherds jostled each other.

"All right, Chief Angel, get ready!"

"I'm ready," Sara said. Suddenly, she let out a bloodcurdling scream! The entire gym shook. Some of the shepherds gasped; others giggled.

Mrs. Smedley nearly dropped her paper. "Hold it!" she said. "What was that all about?"

"I thought I had to scare them!" Sara said.

"No, no," Mrs. Smedley said. "They get terrified just looking at you!"

"No kidding!" Sara said. "What kind of costume do I wear anyhow?"

"These are poor, ignorant shepherds," Mrs. Smedley said. "They've never seen an angel before!"

"Neither have I," Sara said. "I'm not sure I like this!"

"We must move along," Mrs. Smedley said. "Please, just recite your lines."

"Before I do, I have one question," Sara said. "Mrs. Smedley, just what does an angel sound like?"

Everybody giggled.

"I don't know," Mrs. Smedley admitted. "Please, Sara, just say your lines!"

Sara took a big breath and began to read from her paper. "'Do not be afraid,'" she said, in soothing tones. "'I bring you good news.'" Now her voice was cheerful. Every shepherd on the stage stood still and listened as she spoke the line, "'He is Christ the Lord.'" When she came to the end, she sounded like she knew a secret: "'You will find a baby wrapped in cloths and lying in a manger.'"

No one in the gym said a word.

"That was wonderful!" Mrs. Smedley said. "Just wonderful! I knew this would be our finest Christmas pageant!"

Sara was pleased. "Shall I read it again?" she asked. "I've also been practicing saying it with a German accent!"

Mrs. Smedley smiled. "That won't be necessary. This was lovely! Don't change a thing!"

Sara's face almost glowed!

Mrs. Smedley continued. "All right. Now, as the narrator continues, the rest of you angels must step forward to join Sara."

"Suddenly a great company of the heavenly host appeared with the angel, praising God and saying ..." Mrs. Smedley waited.

Actually, without the little angels, the rest of us weren't much of a multitude. I felt really stupid. And then I felt like giggling. Honestly, I couldn't help myself. The harder I tried, the worse it got! Singing was out of the question!

Mrs. Smedley read the narrator's lines again. "Suddenly a great company of the heavenly host appeared with the angel, praising God and saying ..."

My laughter just burst out! It was the kind that's catching. Everybody else just has to join in. They can't help it either! Even Mrs. Smedley laughed.

"Oh, my," she said, finally. "Let's try it again. 'Praising God and saying ...'"

This time we managed to sing our first "Gloria"! But everybody began in a different key. And that set us off again. I laughed until I was weak.

Now Mrs. Smedley got very serious. "I'm glad we're having such a good time. But please, let's remember why we're here. You're Senior Angels, not stand-up comics! You are helping to announce the birth of Jesus!"

She was absolutely right. It wasn't funny. I stared straight ahead without seeing anything. And this time, we made it to the end of our song.

"All right, Chief Shepherd, that's your cue!"

Angela Jones had memorized her part. She took a deep breath and began: "'Let's go to Bethlehem and see this thing that has happened, which the Lord has told us about.'" She never hesitated or made one mistake. Actually, I don't think she even breathed. She just raced ahead, faster and faster, in a high monotone!

"Very good, Angela!" Mrs. Smedley said, at the end. "Now let's try it just a little more slowly!"

Angela tried. Four more times. But, frankly, to me each time sounded exactly the same!

On the fourth try, Mrs. Smedley smiled at her. "That was perfect!" she said. "All right, Shepherds, off the stage! You're on your way to Bethlehem! Use the stairs to your right! Angels, off on the left!"

"I bet you anything Mrs. Smedley has an awful migraine headache," Sara whispered.

A Change
in Family Tradition

When I walked into the church nursery Sunday morning, Mrs. Stone was all smiles. "You're a genius, Katie Hooper!"

"I am?" I figured it had to have something to do with the dog, and I was right!

"We took the whole family to the Animal Shelter yesterday morning," she said. "I don't know if you realized it, but Doris tends to be timid in a new situation. At first, she was afraid to go near the dogs. But Ralph was another story!"

"Was he as good as he sounded in the ad?"

"Even better!" Mrs. Stone said. "He didn't bark or jump or anything. This might sound crazy, but it almost looked as if he smiled at Doris!"

"It doesn't sound crazy to me," I told her. "January smiles all the time!"

"Well, anyhow, it was love at first sight—for all of us!"

"You took Ralph home?"

"Doris wouldn't leave without him! It was either take him home or leave our daughter in the Animal Shelter!"

"And it's working out OK?"

"Better than OK!" Mrs. Stone said. "Ralph will hardly leave Doris's side! He even slept in her room last night!"

"And how about David?"

"Well, you know David!" she laughed. "He's a perfect audience for the two of them!"

"It sounds like Doris is coming out of her room."

"Are you kidding!" her mother said. "She's a different girl!"

I was really pleased. When we piled into Purple Jeep, I couldn't wait to tell my family. "The Stones got a new dog named Ralph," I said. "Mom, they adopted the one you found in the newspaper ad!"

Sara was surprised. "Doris didn't say anything about a dog! But, come to think of it, I didn't have to threaten her once today! It's the best she's acted since I started helping in the toddler nursery!"

"Sara!" Mom said. "You don't really threaten the kids!"

"You do it your way, Mrs. Hooper! Sometimes it's me or them!" Sara grinned. "I just hope they don't spoil our Christmas pageant!"

"The toddlers are in it?" I asked.

"Sure! Who did you think the little angels were, anyway?" Sara asked.

"You mean I have to stand up there on the stage with Doris Stone!" I said. I couldn't believe it. She's just a baby!

"At least there will be a crowd of kids," Jason laughed. "Nobody will see you!"

"Some multitude!" I groaned.

Dad stopped at Sara's and we dropped her off. Suddenly, as we pulled away, I remembered something. It was Family Day again! "Can Sara come over this afternoon to help us trim the tree?"

"No way!" my brother said. "Sara wouldn't know how we do it! She might even throw the tinsel!"

Dad laughed. "She could learn! I had to!"

"Please!" Jason said. "Let's keep it the way we've always done it!"

"It sounds as if you kind of like our traditions after all!" Mom said.

"Trimming a Christmas tree is a very personal thing," Jason said. "It's fun to remember

106

the stories that go with all of the ornaments!"

"Especially your first Christmas after you and Dad got married!" I remembered. "When you strung popcorn and cranberries. And Mom cried because you didn't have any real ornaments!"

"We had one ornament," Mom said. "Don't forget the angel!"

I thought about all the other stories. The ornaments Dad bought Jason and me the years we were born ... The special ones that used to be our grandmother's ... I remembered the stupid ornaments Jason and I made when we were little. Mom kept them just because we made them!

"I just realized that Jason's right!" I said. "Our tree-trimming is very personal! Sara can help her mother trim her own tree!"

Although no one actually used the words "Family Day," it was one of our best ones! When we finished decorating the big tree in the keeping room, we had supper before we started on the small one.

"I never knew you could roast hotdogs in a woodburning stove!" I said.

"Why not? These coals are perfect!" Dad said. "Want another one?"

"I do," Jason said. It figured.

"How come Silent Sam had to put in all that tile?" I asked.

"Everybody has to," Dad said. "It's part of the

fire code. But stoves are safe, as long as you keep the chimney clean."

"I've noticed that the one at Stones' is really hot!" I said.

"Maybe they're just used to a warmer house," Mom said. "Frankly, after the drafts we've been used to, this feels plenty warm to me!"

"Which reminds me," Dad said. "Jason thinks we should go up to Cochrans' for wood. But with Christmas so close now, I'd really rather not take the time to go up there."

"How about asking Sam?" Mom suggested. "I'll bet he knows where we could get enough wood to tide us over."

"Good idea," Dad said. "I'll ask him."

Suddenly, the telephone rang. Jason didn't even look up. Which is why I ran to answer it.

"This is Katie Hooper," I said.

"Are you by any chance Jason's sister?" asked a quiet voice.

"Sure!" I said. "I mean, he's my brother!"

"Do you think your brother could come to the phone?"

"I'll get him!" I ran into the keeping room. "It's for you, Jason! It's a girl!"

"Aha!" Dad laughed. "I told you she'd call!"

"Knock it off!" my brother said. He disappeared into the kitchen.

Mom looked at me. "Is it Allie Meredith?"

"I don't think so."

We didn't have to wait long to find out. Almost immediately, Jason returned. "It's a girl from church. She wants to know if I'm coming to Youth Group. It's at 6:30. Can I go?"

Mom and Dad looked at each other. "I could take you over," Dad said.

"Her parents will pick me up."

"That's fine, Son," Dad said.

Jason disappeared again and returned a second time. He stood, smiling, in the doorway. "If you'll excuse me, I'm going to change my clothes."

I couldn't stop myself from asking. "Was it Jessica? Jessica Hotchkiss?"

Jason shook his head. "No. I didn't really catch her name. She said everybody's been wondering why I haven't come to Youth Group."

"Why haven't you?" I asked.

"I didn't know about it. And, to be honest, nobody invited me!" His smile faded. "You guys don't think I'm deserting the family, do you?"

Mom smiled. "Are you kidding! We've finished decorating the big tree. After all, how many people will it take to trim that little one!"

"Jason, get going!" Dad said.

"Thanks!" Smiling again, he disappeared.

"You know, Elizabeth, we really could end our Family Days by six o'clock," Dad said. "Or I suppose we could switch and schedule them for some evening."

"Something will work out." Mom smiled.

I felt so glad for Jason! Suddenly, I didn't even mind if things changed! Why, we could just start a new tradition! Like Mom said, it will work out! Because my family is special! Really!

Ralph
Saves the Day

It was another busy week. While Mom sewed angel costumes for Sara and me, I had to babysit Amy. Between that and homework, I hardly had any time to knit on Dad's scarf. I decided to take it along to Stones'.

"Have you heard about any dogs?" I asked Mom.

"None!" she said. "Quite a few kittens, but that's it!"

"I called about the Brittany spaniel. Guess what? Three hundred dollars! What am I going to do?"

"Smart dogs with papers are always expensive!" Mom said. "Maybe you should just think of something else to get her."

"It's too bad I couldn't have Ralph!" I said. "He sounds perfect!"

"He is perfect—for Doris," Mom reminded me. "If M. is supposed to have a dog, the Lord will make sure you hear about it!"

I remembered something. "What happened with the firewood?"

"Dad and Jason are planning to go up to Cochrans' after all. Nothing else worked out."

"Mom, I wish I could stop thinking about Ralph," I said.

"Why don't you call the Animal Shelter? Maybe Ralph has a brother!"

It was an excellent idea! I wondered why I hadn't thought of it! But when I called, the man told me Ralph was a one-of-a-kind! He did say they'll keep an eye out for me.

From the time Mr. Stone picked me up Friday night, all he could talk about was Ralph! "Doris isn't the only one who loves him," he said. "We all do! Actually, Ralph reminds me of the dog I had as a child!"

I could hardly wait to meet Ralph! He and Doris were in the living room when we got there. But, to be honest, he didn't look loving to me! As I walked in, Ralph did not smile. He stood up, took one look at me, and growled!

"It's OK, Ralph," Doris said. "Katie's our friend!"

Ralph relaxed. So did I. He's large, and he looks mostly like a German shepherd. His fur is tan underneath, with black frosting.

"Come here, Ralph!" Mr. Stone said. Ralph came. I was impressed. But I didn't pet him. I left that to Mr. Stone.

When Mrs. Stone came in wearing her red dress, Ralph went and stood looking up at her. "Don't be sad, Boy! I'll come back!" She leaned down and stroked his broad head.

"Come here, Ralph!" Doris said. "Let's show Katie your trick!" When she threw the ball, the dog started after it. And David, in his playpen, laughed out loud.

"Isn't it something!" Mrs. Stone said. "Ralph has brought us all together!"

Frankly, I thought Mr. and Mrs. Stone would never leave! I got to thinking that if things get any more chummy, I just might be out of a job! But finally the parents headed off.

"Let David stay up and watch!" Doris begged. "Don't make him go to bed!"

"It's time," I said, picking up the baby. (By the way, when I changed his diaper this time, I laid a clean one over him—just in case!)

"Doris, do you want to play a game?"

She shook her head. "Katie, I hope you won't feel bad!"

Later, she didn't even want me to hear her

prayers. "It's private," she said, with a solemn face. "Only Ralph can listen!"

I smiled as I left girl and dog together in her room. Leaving the door open a crack, I headed upstairs. The family room, with its woodburning stove, was too warm for me.

I sat on the living room sofa and began to knit on Dad's scarf. As I knitted, I thought about my father—how much I love him and how proud I am of him! I thought about Sara and how fortunate I am! Then I told the Lord I'm glad He's a Father to all the kids who don't have one!

Suddenly, just when I got to the end of a row, I heard loud barking! It scared me and I jumped! I leaned over the banister and called down softly, "It's OK, Ralph! Be still! You'll wake the children!"

Ralph stopped. I was just about to sit down again when he started barking louder than ever. Oh, no! I'd have to go downstairs! I had no idea how I could make him be quiet!

As I started down, I turned on the light. I realized that Ralph was in the family room. And that's when I heard the noise! It was the sound of loud popping and crackling. What in the world? "The stove!" I said out loud. "It just has to be the stove!"

There was no time to call my mother. There was no time to call anybody. I just knew I had to get the children out of the house! Once I was sure the children were safe, somebody could figure this out!

"Come on, Ralph!" I said. "Let's go get Doris!" He stopped barking and led the way down the hall.

I didn't want to scare her. But I didn't have forever, either! "Doris!" My voice was incredibly calm! "Wake up!"

"What's happening?" she asked.

"Quick!" I said, softly. "I think something's wrong with the stove! We're going outside!"

"Can Ralph come too?" she asked.

"Of course! Let's go!"

She was wearing one of those blanket things with feet, and it was hard for her to walk. I took her hand, and we started out.

As we passed the family room and climbed the steps, Doris heard the noise. "Katie, I'm scared!" she said.

"We're almost out!" I fumbled with the door lock. It sounds dumb, but I heard my cheerful voice saying, "At least it isn't snowing!"

I almost dragged Doris to the middle of the yard. "Where's my brother?" she remembered. "We have to save David!"

"I'm getting him now," I told her. "Doris, I want you to stay right here and wait for me!"

"I can't!" she sobbed. "I'm afraid!"

115

"Tell the Lord about it," I told her. "Ralph can stay right here with you! He'll listen while you pray! I'll be right back!"

I raced to the door and up the half-flight of stairs. For a second, everything in the living room looked so normal that I wondered if I was doing the right thing! But this was no time to think! I turned and ran down the hall and into the nursery.

I switched on the light. It didn't take me more than a few seconds to wrap David in a blanket and carry him outside.

Now, Ralph was barking again, and Doris was hanging onto him and crying.

Before I could figure out what to do next, a neighbor's door opened and a man called out, "Is something wrong?"

"Help me!" I called. "Please help me! I think there's something wrong with the woodburning stove!"

He turned and yelled, "Ann! Call the fire department!" Then he ran out to where we were huddled. "Did you see any flames?"

"No. But there's an awful popping and crackling noise!"

"It has to be the chimney!" He ran toward the house. "Wait here! I'm going to try to close the damper!"

Lights started going on, and people started

coming out. And, in the distance, we heard a fire siren!

"Katie!" Doris said. "Is my house really going to burn down?"

"I hope not!" I told her. "Lord! Please don't let it burn! And keep that man safe!"

"Children! Come with me!" said a woman's soft voice. "Where are the Stones?"

"They're gone for the evening," I said. "I'm the babysitter."

Actually, I missed most of the exciting part. I didn't get to see even one fireman! Because we were stuck in the house next door.

"What's your name?" asked the neighbor.

"I'm Katie Hooper," I said. "I guess you already know Doris and David and Ralph!"

"You're a real heroine, Katie Hooper!" said the nice lady.

Suddenly, it hit me. Everyone really was safe! What a relief! Then I couldn't help it. I started to cry!

Later, as Dad was driving me home in Purple Jeep, I cried again. It probably sounds stupid. But that's when I remembered that I had left my father's unfinished scarf in Stones' living room!

Dress Rehearsal

Being a heroine sure gives you an appetite! At breakfast the next morning, I ate seven pancakes!

"You won't be able to sing!" Mom laughed.

"Tell me again what to do if we get a fire in our chimney," Jason said.

"We don't have to worry," Mom said. "Sam made sure our chimney was clean and in good condition when he installed our wood stove."

"When Stones bought their house, their stove was already in use," Dad said. "Nobody told them that burning wood causes creosote to build up in a chimney. That's what caught fire last night."

"You're sure their house is OK?" I asked.

"It's fine," Dad said. "There isn't even any smoke damage. Thanks to you, Katie!"

"Don't forget Ralph!" I said. "If Ralph hadn't barked, I might not have noticed it."

I didn't have much time to bask in glory! If we didn't get going, we'd be late for dress rehearsal of our pageant! The show must go on!

"I'm so nervous! I've been up since five!" Sara said, when she got in the car. "By the way, did your mother finish my costume?"

I nodded. "It's in this box. Guess what, Sara? I finally had another adventure!"

"You did?"

"Katie's a heroine!" Jason said. "Stones had a chimney fire last night, and Katie saved the children!"

"It's my adventure!" I said. "Let me tell it, Jason!" Actually, telling it took most of the way to church. And I had to rush the part about the fire engine.

"Weren't you scared?" Sara asked. "I'd have been petrified!"

"It's worse thinking about it now," I said. "Last night I just did what I had to do!"

"Katie, you really are a heroine!" Sara said. "If they do a TV special about you, maybe I can play the part of Katie Hooper!"

"That wouldn't be fair!" I told her. "They should let me do it! Sara, you can't be me!"

Dad just laughed and shook his head. "Good luck, kids! Call me when you're finished."

Inside, at one end of the noisy gym, Mrs. Smedley was trying to maintain some order. "All right, everybody!" she yelled. "If you didn't come in your costume, slip it on now! We'll begin in five minutes!"

"I don't see any little angels," I told Sara. "Are you sure they're going to be in it?"

"I'm sure," Sara said. "How do I look?"

Actually, I nearly laughed out loud. But I knew I couldn't. Unless I controlled myself, I'd ruin the pageant! So I just ignored her red hair pointing out in every direction, the checked shirt sticking out at the neck, the pink jogging shoes, and the silly smile on Sara's face.

"You look like an angel!" I said. "At least you will when you get your halo!"

"Katie, you look hilarious!" she told me. Now the gym was settling down. The Three Kings, wearing their bathrobes, marched single file around the room.

At the far end of the gym, I saw Jessica Hotchkiss and my brother. Jessica, with her blue robe pulled up inside her rope belt, was shooting free throws! Jason and some of the shepherds were cheering her on. I smiled as one of the shepherds gave Mary a high five!

"All right!" Mrs. Smedley called. "Please give

me your attention! Unfortunately, Mr. Stone, our narrator, won't be here again today. He has a good excuse! Last night his house nearly burned down! I'm proud to tell you that one of our Senior Angels saved the family from tragedy! Let's give a hand to Katie Hooper!"

Everybody looked at me and cheered. Those standing near me wanted to hear what happened.

"Katie can tell us about it some other time," Mrs. Smedley said. "Don't forget, this is our last rehearsal before the actual pageant! Today we'll take it straight through from the top!"

With Mrs. Smedley reading the narrator's part, we began. "In those days Caesar Augustus issued a decree that a census should be taken of the entire Roman world. . . ."

From the right, Jessica and Jason entered. My brother looked embarrassed, and she looked hot. They trudged silently across the stage to the inn without Mrs. Smedley's interruption.

Once Mary and Joseph got to the inn, nothing happened. "Mark Mahoney, are you here?" Mrs. Smedley called. "You're supposed to be on the stage behind that door!"

"Roger!" said Mark Mahoney. "How will I know when Mary and Joseph get here?"

"Joseph, you can knock softly," Mrs. Smedley said. "All right, let's go!"

Joseph knocked softly, and the wall nearly fell down. Mary giggled.

"There's no room in the inn!" Mark Mahoney yelled. He said it so loud that Mary and Joseph jumped. Everybody laughed. Everybody except Mrs. Smedley.

"All right," she said. "Will someone please start the record! As the music plays 'It Came Upon the Midnight Clear,' I want all the angels and shepherds to take their places. Quietly."

I followed Sara up the stairs. I didn't even look at her. No one laughed. Especially not me!

Now Mrs. Smedley was reading: "An angel of the Lord appeared to them, and the glory of the Lord shone around them, and they were terrified."

This time, Sara didn't scream. What a relief! The shepherds managed to look kind of scared anyway.

But now nothing happened. It was time for Sara's lines. But she just stood there. Finally, I gave her a little poke. Now Sara looked more scared than the shepherds!

"All right," Mrs. Smedley said softly. "Go ahead, Sara."

"'Do not be afraid. He is Christ the Lord!'" Sara said.

"You left out the good news." I whispered.

"I've got good news for you!" Sara said.

Mrs. Smedley rescued her. "All right, Sara," she said, "try it from the beginning. 'Do not be afraid. . . .'"

"'Do not be afraid,'" Sara said. She was very dramatic. But she couldn't remember what came next!

"'I bring you good news . . .'"

"'I bring you good news of great joy that will be for all the people. . . .'"

I started to breath again.

"'This will be a sign to you: You will find a baby wrapped in cloths and lying in a manger,'" Sara recited.

"Sara, you left out 'He is Christ the Lord,'" Mrs. Smedley said.

"I thought I already said that!" Sara said. "This is really embarrassing!"

"Maybe you should just read your lines again today," Mrs. Smedley suggested.

"OK," Sara said. "I have it right here!" She pulled out her piece of paper and read the lines with great feeling. But somehow nobody felt as good about it as last week. In fact, the shepherds looked downright nervous.

"It's going to be all right," Mrs. Smedley said afterwards. "That can happen to anybody! At the real performance, Sara will do it perfectly! All right now, let's hear from the Heavenly Host!"

Actually, the angels had to perform without halos. Whoever's making all the halos didn't get finished. But our "Glorias" sounded pretty good anyway. And we didn't laugh! Mrs. Smedley seemed pleased.

When all the shepherds and angels got to the manger, it was so crowded that nobody could even see Mary and Joseph! So Mrs. Smedley made us all kneel down. And then we all had to clear out before the Three Kings got there.

"It's still a little rough," Mrs. Smedley told everybody. "But I'd be worried if it weren't! Dress rehearsals are always like this! It's a sign that the actual performance will be perfect!"

"I hope Mrs. Smedley knows what she's talking about!" Sara said. "If not, my career is ruined!"

A Dog for Mayblossom

Sometimes I wonder if teachers are born without any Christmas spirit! Just before the holiday recess, Ms. Allen piled on the homework! Sara's teacher was just as bad. We could hardly wait for the first day of vacation.

"In the morning, let's go shopping!" Sara said. "Are you all done?"

"Nearly. I finished Dad's scarf last night. Boy, am I glad my knitting didn't burn up!"

"Afterwards, maybe you could help me practice my pageant part," she said. "I'm getting worried! At home I know my lines perfectly. But when I try to give my part some meaning, I forget where I am! Could you be the shepherds?"

"I suppose so."

I didn't tell Sara I was worried too. It was nearly Christmas, and I still hadn't found a dog for M.! Maybe I could stop in at the Animal Shelter. If they saw me in person, they'd know I really meant business!

And then last night it happened. During supper, a man called from the Animal Shelter. "Are you the girl looking for a dog like Ralph?" asked a man's voice.

"I am! Did you really find another Ralph?"

The man laughed. "Not exactly. This one's just a puppy. And it's female!"

"I'll be downtown tomorrow," I said. "Can you save the dog for me?"

"We'll be open until noon," the man said.

I was so excited I could hardly stand it! But in front of my family, I acted real cool.

The next phone call was for Jason, who came back to the table smiling. "Some guys from Youth Group want me to go tobogganing in the morning. They said it's supposed to snow tonight."

"I thought you were going up to Cochrans' with your father," Mom remembered. "Isn't that when you're getting the firewood?"

"Oh, no! I forgot!" Jason said.

"I can handle it myself." Dad smiled. "It sounds like a good chance for you to get to know some Christian kids."

"Thanks, Dad!" Jason beamed.

Before I went to bed, I wrapped my presents. They all looked pretty much the same. Actually, they even *felt* pretty much the same. It isn't easy to disguise four similar scarves!

Well, it snowed all right! Did it ever! Sara called to say I'd have to go downtown alone. She would be clearing driveways.

"I'd like you to come to Cochrans' with me, Katie," Dad said. "On a day like this, I don't want to drive Sam's truck up there by myself."

"Sorry, I can't," I said. "I have plans."

"Well, you can change them," he said. "With Christmas so close, your mother can't spare the time. And Jason's all set to go with his friends."

"It isn't fair," I said. "Can't you drive up later?"

"I told Sam I'd have his truck back," Dad said. "Katie, I don't intend to argue about it."

There was no point in running upstairs to Mom. Dad and Mom always back each other up. And we kids are expected to obey both of them. This isn't just a Hooper family tradition. Actually, this rule is right in the Bible!

"When will we be home?" I asked.

"It depends on the roads. Let's get started!"

It was slow going through town. I almost could have run in to see little Ralph! "Dad, on the way home, can we stop in town?"

"Sure." Dad winked at me. "Christmas secret?"

128

"I guess you could call it that," I said.

After we got a few miles north of Woodland Park, the roads were much better. "It isn't as bad as I thought it would be," Dad said. "But you never know, especially in a borrowed vehicle. I thought I'd need help seeing the road."

Once I got a better attitude, I began to enjoy the trip. Lately, I haven't had the chance to do much with my father. "The view is spectacular, isn't it?" I said.

"Too bad I can't stop to paint!"

"I wish we had time to stop at Mayblossom's." I realized we'd be going right near her cabin.

Dad smiled. "Did you know she's been coming every week to our Sunday-school class?"

"No, I didn't. That's one trouble with working in the nursery. By the time people pick up their babies, I don't get to see anybody else."

"I bet M. will come to the pageant!" he said.

"It could be awful," I told him. "Sara keeps forgetting her lines."

Dad smiled. "I used to have a terrible time memorizing anything! I'll pray for her!"

It's been years since I visited the sheep ranch. Someone else owned it then. Jason's the one who knows his way around here now. Before we moved to town, he worked for Cochrans!

"Good morning!" Mr. Cochran said. "Right on time!"

"We had more snow in Woodland Park," Dad said. "I wasn't sure we'd make it so fast!"

"Jason didn't come?"

"He said to tell you he had a chance to go tobogganing. He'd like to come after Christmas."

"Whenever he can come is fine!" Mr. Cochran smiled. "And you must be Katie!"

I smiled back. "I met your wife last summer!"

"She told me," Mr. Cochran said. "She's in the house. Why don't you run in and see her while I help your father load the wood."

Mrs. Cochran met me at the door. "Come on in, Katie! Can I give you something to eat? How about a Christmas cookie?"

"Sure!" I said. "Jason always told us you're a good cook!"

"Is he helping load the wood?"

I shook my head. "He went tobogganing with some kids from Youth Group. Oh, you have a puppy!"

"It's left from Gretta's litter," Mrs. Cochran said. "They were born right after you moved."

"I remember!" I said. "Jason was planning to bring me to see the new puppies."

"Well, Katie, you got something even better! Amy's certainly a darling baby!"

I knelt down. The puppy wanted to play. "What kind is it? I thought you were getting those dogs that look just like the sheep!"

"Oh, no!" Mrs. Cochran smiled. "Komondors are great with the sheep. But they don't make good pets. This one's a German shepherd."

"No kidding!"

"We sold Gretta's other puppies, but so far we haven't been able to find a home for this one."

"How come?"

"There's a problem with the way her bite lines up. Actually, she needs orthodontia!"

"Braces?" I said. "For a dog!"

Mrs. Cochran laughed. "Something like that. There's a vet in Denver that can help her. But we can't sell her with papers. Most people want a perfect dog!"

I couldn't believe my ears! "Guess what?" I said. "I think I know somebody! Have you met Mayblossom McDuff?"

"The one who bought your cabin?" she asked. "I've been planning to get over there, but I just haven't had time. You say she wants a dog?"

"I've been trying to find a dog I could give her for Christmas!" I remembered something. "I found out that dogs with papers are expensive!"

Mrs. Cochran smiled. "Actually, I was hoping to give the puppy to someone who would have the dental work done! But we haven't found anyone like that."

I was so excited I could hardly stand it! "I

really think Mayblossom McDuff would be perfect! Could she come over to see the dog?"

"That sounds like a good idea!" Mrs. Cochran said. "A pet is very personal! It's not really wise to try to pick one out for somebody else!"

I could hardly stand it. I excused myself and ran outside. "Guess what, Dad? Cochrans are giving away a darling German shepherd puppy!"

"I know," Dad said. "Mr. Cochran was just telling me about it. But we don't have room in town! It's too bad we don't know somebody else who wants one!"

"I do, Dad!" I said. "I think I have the perfect person!"

We Give Our Performance

"Katie, the puppy's perfect! I'm so excited! This is the most wonderful Christmas present I've ever received in my life!" Mayblossom McDuff was laughing and hugging me.

To be honest, I felt almost as hyper myself! "There's only one trouble," I told her. "The dog was supposed to be a surprise!"

M. laughed her tinkling laugh. "What are you talking about? I've never been so surprised in my life!" She kept stroking the dog.

"Actually, no one's happier or more surprised than I am!" said Mrs. Cochran. "I couldn't have asked for a more wonderful home for Gretta's puppy! And you live so close that we can still see her!"

"Look!" M. said. "She wants to play!"

"Do you want to take the puppy home with you now?" Mrs. Cochran asked.

Mayblossom winked at me. "No, I can't! She's a Christmas gift! Do you think I could pick her up Christmas morning? That will give me time to get ready for her arrival."

"Maybe you can bring the dog along when you come for Christmas dinner," I said.

She grinned. "My plan exactly!" she said. "Don't tell anyone! Won't they be surprised!"

"I'll ask my father not to say anything! When it comes to secrets, he's the greatest!"

Mayblossom laughed. "There's only one problem! I'm not sure I can wait until Christmas!"

"By the way, are you coming to the pageant?" I asked. "Did you know I'm a Senior Angel?"

"I'll be there!" M. said. She turned to Mrs. Cochran. "Would you and your husband like to ride down with me?"

"Jason's in it too!" I said. "Don't tell him I told you, but he's going to be Joseph!"

Mrs. Cochran laughed. "It sounds like a performance we shouldn't miss!"

"Jason and I don't actually have speaking parts!" I said. I didn't mention Sara. If she blows it, the less we talk about it, the better!

Dad stuck his head in the door. "I'm ready to leave, Katie. I want to get the truck back."

Seated in the front of the truck, I turned to my father. "Dad, please don't tell anybody that M. is getting the dog!"

Smiling, he got a stupid look on his face. "M. who? What dog?" I knew the secret was safe!

On the night of the Christmas pageant, my father made two trips to the church. Jason, Sara, and I had to be there early. Sara's mother was coming later with my parents and Amy.

At night, the gym looks entirely different. The light was dim, and Christmas carols played softly. Even the kids talked in hushed tones. Partly it was quiet because the Little Angels were off in another room!

"Is my halo straight?" Sara asked.

"Pretty straight," I said. "How about mine?"

Sara and the Senior Angels get to wear halos that are a creative marvel! They took so long to make that the smaller angels didn't get any. Instead, the toddlers got stuck with wearing pieces of tinsel wrapped around their little heads!

Since it was elastic, the headband part of our halos fit everybody. But if you weren't careful, the wand that held up the round halo would droop down. To be honest, they looked hilarious! But I couldn't let myself even think about that!

"Are you OK?" I asked Sara.

"I'm praying," she told me.

"Right," I said. Frankly, I've never seen Sara so subdued. I realized that if I had a long speaking part, I'd be scared to death! Silently, I stood next to her and watched all the folding chairs fill with people. I was excited to see M. and the Cochrans filing into the fourth row.

And then the pageant began.

Actually, before we really started, everybody sang two carols, and there was a choral reading, and an offering, and the minister prayed. But then Mr. Stone took his place at the left of the stage and began to read: "In those days Caesar Augustus issued a decree that a census should be taken of the entire Roman world...."

Mr. Stone's voice was, of course, entirely different from Mrs. Smedley's. Something about it made me listen as if I'd never heard the story before! And as Mary and Joseph made their way across to the inn, I even forgot it was Jason!

I watched as Mary and Joseph were turned away at the inn. The scenery stayed put, and the innkeeper's line was flawless. Now Mary and Joseph headed for the manger and sat down.

And then the shepherds and angels heard what we were waiting for—the first notes of "It Came Upon the Midnight Clear."

Unfortunately, Mr. Stone had never been to a rehearsal, so he didn't know how long it takes for everybody to get on the stage! He just continued reading: "And there were shepherds living out in the fields nearby, keeping watch over their flocks at night. An angel ..."

Meanwhile, the shepherds and angels were still waiting to go up the steps to the stage! Mrs. Smedley tried to signal Mr. Stone to stop. Finally, she had to step onto the stage and whisper in his ear. Only then did he quit reading!

Well, at last we stood in our places. But then the whole production had to wait until the teachers brought out the Little Angels!

They looked adorable! One tiny boy with tinsel hanging over one eye saw his parents and waved! Naturally, everybody laughed. A smiling Doris Stone recognized me and ran to take my hand! At last, when the Heavenly Host was complete on the stage, everyone clapped!

Mrs. Smedley signaled Mr. Stone to begin again. Now, when he got to the "glory" part, somebody shone a spotlight in our eyes!

"An angel of the Lord appeared to them, and the glory of the Lord shone around them, and they were terrified. But the angel said to them ..."

I held my breath as Sara began to speak. So did all the other actors!

We needn't have worried. Sara's voice was clear and steady and full of meaning:

"Do not be afraid. I bring you good news of great joy that will be for all the people. Today in the town of David a Savior has been born to you; he is Christ the Lord. This will be a sign to you: You will find a baby wrapped in cloths and lying in a manger."

As Sara spoke, you could have heard a pin drop! And by the time the angels began to sing our "Glorias," I felt almost as if I really were out there in that field!

Now, as the Chief Shepherd spoke, the stage lights grew dim. Everyone squeezed in and knelt down around Mary and Joseph. But when the light shone again on the manger, everyone gasped. I couldn't believe it! Lying there, on a small blanket, was a real baby!

It took a minute for the people in the audience to realize what was happening. Some people stood up so they could see better. Mrs. Smedley came out and led the Little Angels closer to the manger. It was so sweet I nearly cried!

Suddenly, the gym was electrified by Doris's voice. "Wow! Wait until I tell my mother! Jesus looks exactly like my baby brother!"

The place went up for grabs! It must have taken at least ten minutes before the Wise-men could do their thing!

Afterwards, we realized that Mrs. Smedley had been right all along! Everyone in the church said it was our best Christmas pageant ever!

Our family and friends, except for Jason, stood together in line for punch and cookies. Frankly, I had no idea where my brother was.

"You were wonderful, Sara!" Dad told her. "And you make a beautiful angel, Katie!"

Mayblossom smiled and gave me a big hug. We both giggled as my halo slipped down.

"But Sara was the star!" I said.

Sara Wilcox smiled and reached up with her left hand to steady her halo. "Thanks, Katie, but that's not right," she said. "I wasn't really the star! The star of the show was the baby! After all, he's the Son of God! And you can't get any higher than that!"

Everyone smiled. "Out of the mouths of babes," Dad said.

Some Things I'll Always Remember

This was my best Christmas ever! Sometimes when you look forward to something so much, it turns out to be disappointing. But that has never happened to me on Christmas!

My family's celebration starts on Christmas Eve. That's when we have a birthday party for Jesus, complete with ice cream and cake! This year I still got to blow out the candles. Soon Amy will start doing it. But I won't mind.

We decided to hang our stockings at the fireplace in the keeping room. They're red and green felt with our names on them. Even Dad has one! This year Mom added a new stocking for Amy.

On Christmas morning, Jason and I are supposed to stay in bed until our parents get up. But we have a secret! Whoever wakes up first wakes the other one! Then we always sneak down together, look at the boxes under the tree, feel our stockings, and tiptoe back to bed to wait for the others to get up!

After Mom and Dad wake up, we go downstairs again. Jason and I always act real surprised! Then everyone sings "Joy to the World" and we open our stockings. On Christmas, we eat homemade coffeecake in our pajamas.

This year, we went to church. I sat in the seventh row with Dad, Mom, Jason, and Amy. Sara and her mother also sat with us. The minister reminded everyone that Baby Jesus grew up! Actually, He's the same person who died on the cross for our sins! That's what being a Savior means!

After we got home, we sat around the wood stove and gave each other our gifts! Dad always gets a big kick out of handing them out.

Not to brag, but the scarves I knitted were sensational! My family loved them! In wrapping them, I had mixed up the tags, so Amy got a green scarf, and Jason got Amy's pink one! That gave us a big laugh!

Dad painted watercolor pictures of our old cabin for Jason and me! Mom made me a new blue jumper! And my brother surprised everyone with birds he carved out of wood! We didn't even know he knew how to do it!

By afternoon, the wonderful smell of turkey filled the house again, and we waited for the arrival of our new "family"! This time, January never howled once! "Of course not," Mom laughed. "Even January knows you don't sing the 'Star Spangled Banner' on Christmas!"

Sara Wilcox arrived wearing pantyhose and new black shoes with little heels! She got my name in the draw and couldn't wait until we opened our gifts! She gave me cool ski mittens!

The last person to get here was Mayblossom McDuff. She came in a shiny four-wheel drive she bought herself for Christmas! The new puppy, wearing a red bow around its neck, was the center of attention! M. told everybody that the puppy is a gift from me! By the way, the dog's name is Noel!

During dinner, Silent Sam asked my brother if we open our gifts on Christmas Eve. "No, we always open them Christmas Day," Jason told him. Then he winked at Mom and Dad. "Actually," he said, "it's a Hooper Family Tradition!"

Well, that's about it! I can't believe that Christmas is over! Actually, I'm already looking forward to next year!

Fiction for Girls

by

Jane Sorenson

It's Me, Jennifer
It's Your Move, Jennifer
Jennifer's New Life
Jennifer Says Goodbye
Boy Friend
Once Upon a Friendship
Fifteen Hands
In Another Land
The New Pete
Out with the In Crowd
Another Jennifer
Family Crisis

Hi, I'm Katie Hooper
Home Sweet Haunted Home
Happy Birth Day
Honor Roll
First Job
Angels on Holiday
The New Me
Left Behind